Yali, dressed now in a pantsuit of ecru lace, shrugged elegant shoulders. "We do have eagles here," she said, cool and amused, "but, Dusa, they aren't giants. You might see one in a treetop, or circling in the sky—but *walking*? They hop if they have to, but they'd much rather fly. Your eyes must have tricked you. The light is so bright here, it's not surprising."

Dusa felt about ten years old. "I guess," she said, doubtfully. She was silent. The others were silent. Dusa, inexperienced in such silences, broke it first. "So, tell me about the oak trees. Are they"—she remembered her teacher's phrase—"old-growth forest?"

Yali and Teno both pounced. Had she gone into the trees? That was dangerous, hadn't they told her to be careful? What did she see? What did she find?

"No snakes, thank goodness," said Dusa, surprised by a sudden burst of angry energy. "Not on the ground, and not in my head, and just as well—I wouldn't want anything to make me jump when I was on those cliffs." She changed the subject for a second time.

"I did find a big stone," she said quietly, "all on end, like a giant tombstone, I thought, even though I know it was silly to think that. I'm sure nobody is buried there."

"The old stories say a body *is* buried there," said Teno slowly, "a body without a head."

"Teno," Yali scolded, "that's no way to cure Dusa's nightmares. Don't let her scare you, Dusa. There's nothing to be scared about."

"True enough," said Teno. "But don't believe everything you hear, Dusa—or everything you see, either," she added, looking directly at the startled girl.

SNAKE DREAMER

Priscilla Galloway

LAUREL-LEAF BOOKS

Published by
Dell Laurel-Leaf
an imprint of
Random House Children's Books
a division of Random House, Inc.
1540 Broadway
New York, New York 10036

Visit Priscilla Galloway's Web site! http//webhome.idirect.com/~gallcom
Visit us on the Web! www.randomhouse.com/teens

Educators and librarians, for a variety of teaching tools, visit us at
www.randomhouse.com/teachers

ISBN 0-440-22017-3

RL: 5.4

Reprinted by arrangement with Delacorte Press

Printed in the United States of America

March 2000

10 9 8 7 6 5 4 3 2 1

OPM

To my daughter, Noël,
and my granddaughters,
Leigh, Laney and Season,
with love

Somebody was screaming. Twenty or thirty snakes twisted about, hissing loudly. They were furious; the screamer was consumed by their rage.

The little black snake with the sapphire stripes stared down into Dusa's right eye. Its ruby tongue flicked in and out with lightning speed. The big golden snake curled itself around the girl's face. It felt dry, slightly leathery. Its seeking head reared in menace on Dusa's other side.

Dusa's own dark curly head was pillowed on the bodies of snakes; they undulated wildly beneath her. Her nostrils curled with their musty odor. Her eyes ached with the strain of focusing on the two visible serpents, while she tried at the same time to extend her peripheral vision to see the others. Why were the snakes so angry? What unseen threat did they feel? Dusa's throat ached with her screams.

Pearl Thrasman jumped out of bed and ran into her daughter's room. Dusa's back arched suddenly. Her arms and legs jerked violently. Spittle drooled from her mouth.

The screams continued, with barely a pause for breath. Pearl threw her arms around the thrashing body. Dusa's fist shot out, connecting almost professionally with her mother's chin. With scarcely a pause, Dusa's two hands closed around her mother's neck.

Pearl struggled for air. In her panic, she managed to pry Dusa's fingers away. Dizzy and sick, Pearl fought for breath. If nothing changed, she realized suddenly, Dusa would kill her one day.

CHAPTER 1

"It's not epilepsy," said the doctor. He rattled the curtain around the hospital bed and the adjacent chair, enclosing the mother and his young patient in spurious privacy. He looked down almost angrily at the quiet mother, then at the skinny teenager with the huge deep blue eyes. He wanted very badly to be able to tell her she was cured.

"Not epilepsy," he repeated. "That's the good news. The bad news"—he paused—"the bad news is that we don't know what it is. All our tests don't tell us. You're better, Dusa, no thanks to us.

"We're sending you home. I hope you don't have any more seizures—er, episodes." He frowned; his medical vocabulary had no satisfactory term to describe Dusa's attacks. "Maybe the therapy has helped to chase away the nightmares; you certainly haven't assaulted anybody here." He glanced apologetically at the girl's mother; Pearl had asked him not to remind Dusa about the stranglehold.

"Medication, anything we've tried, has been a mistake, hasn't it?"

The girl in the bed shuddered, nodding.

The doctor went on, "I've made out your discharge papers, Dusa. When do you want to go?"

The girl looked out at the brilliant blue late-September sky. For more than a week, the snakes had been quiet; it was easy to pretend they would be quiet forever. "Now," said Dusa. "No more needles, no more CAT scans, let me out of here. Now!"

A warm smile lit up her mother's ordinary, pleasant face. Exhaustion, for the moment, disappeared. Pearl straightened her shoulders, then dug into a large black vinyl handbag, producing a small notebook and pen. Her pen ready, she asked, "What should we do if it starts again?"

Dusa shivered. Her euphoria had vanished.

The doctor threw up his hands. "Keep to a routine," he replied. "Minimize stress. Be careful, Mrs. Thrasman, what else can I say? Shall I tell the nurses you'll be ready to leave in half an hour?"

"Wait a minute." Pearl shook her head. Her chin still felt bruised from Dusa's unintentional punch; her throat still hurt with every mouthful she swallowed. "There's nothing new in any of that. Dusa's been here for two weeks. You don't know what's wrong with her, exactly, I understand that. But—have you no help for us, nothing at all? Is that what you're telling me?" She could hear her voice becoming loud and shrill.

Dr. Andrews grimaced. "I don't know when I've been so frustrated," he said. "We've already got two other opinions about Dusa, excellent doctors, top specialists. We did some really exotic blood tests for Dr. Chan, but nothing showed up. You know about this. It was only an outside chance, she told us, but worth a try. Dr. Wright couldn't suggest anything new."

Pearl shook her head. "You have tried, Dr. Andrews. We know you've tried." Her shoulders slumped.

"I don't believe this!" Dusa knew in another minute she would begin to scream, or to cry. Whichever it was, she didn't think she would be able to stop. She glared at the doctor. "Are you giving up on me? Sure you've tried, but you're *not doing anything*!" Her voice was almost a shriek. "I want to go home, I want to go to school and I never, ever want to hit my mom again, even in my sleep."

The doctor and her mother turned to her, her mother's mouth falling open in shock. Dr. Andrews was a big, burly man. He looked as if he would be more at home on a football field than in this hospital room, though Dusa knew that his square hands were gentle, his stubby fingers delicate in their touch. Now he blushed, his light blue eyes showing bluer in his crimson face. "There could be something," he began, and stopped.

"Well?" challenged Dusa.

"I'm not recommending this," said Dr. Andrews. "You're pushing me, Dusa."

Dusa's sapphire eyes flashed dangerously.

"Okay, okay, I know how you feel."

Dusa's dark eyebrows lifted in disbelief.

Dr. Andrews glared at her; then he threw up his hands and laughed. "What's the big deal? I'm on your side, Dusa. I don't like those snakes either. There's a TV program tonight, I saw the ad. I'm going to watch. You watch too, and then we'll talk. Remember, I don't know anything about it, just the little bit I saw, and it looked like crazy stuff—but then, it's pretty crazy stuff we're dealing with."

"So now I'm crazy." Dusa's face was still stiff with anger.

Dr. Andrews shook his head. "I must be losing it," he grumbled. "No, Dusa, that's not what I meant. There are some bizarre elements in your illness, we agree about that, that's all I meant. End of story. Period."

"What is the program about?" Pearl interposed quietly.

"That's all I'm going to say," said Dr. Andrews stiffly. "Discovery Channel at seven o'clock. And I'll probably kick myself for not keeping my mouth shut."

Pearl smiled uncertainly. "Thank you," she said. "We'll watch, won't we, Dusa?"

"Sure." Dusa's voice was flat. "We'll watch." She sat up briskly and swung her legs over the side of the bed. "Let's get out of here," she said. "If we hurry, I can go back to school this afternoon."

"Do you think you should?" asked her mother. She looked at the doctor.

"Sure," he said. "If that's what you want."

Dusa nodded.

"Go for it, then. Why not? It's a beautiful day."

"All right," said Pearl. "In that case, I'll go back to the office. My boss will be thrilled, even if I'm not exactly dressed for business." She looked down dubiously at her worn beige corduroy pants and grubby once-white sneakers. "Thank you, Doctor, we'll be in touch." Dusa's small suitcase was quickly packed. Her mom paid the bill, a small balance for the telephone and TV rental, and off they went.

When the door opened at six-thirty, Dusa was stirring a pot on the stove with her right hand and holding the telephone with her left. "Mom's home," she told her friend, "I'll phone you later. Thanks for your notes."

Pearl's steps were slow, but a smile brightened her tired face as she came into the kitchen. Dusa handed her the phone, and she hung it back on the wall. "It's sure been funny, having the phone to myself." Pearl grinned. "I didn't really want to get used to it. What smells so good?"

"Spaghetti," said Dusa cheerfully. "The sauce is a Dusa creation. I chopped up some chicken and added it to the stuff in the no-name can."

"How was school?"

"Okay. I've got a pile of catching up to do."

"So, how do you feel?"

"Tired," said Dusa, "but okay so far. Tonight will be the test, won't it, the first test." She was serious now. "Nobody will be coming around at the crack of dawn to take my blood. Mom, it's good to be home. I hope I don't wake you up, and I sure hope I don't beat you up, me and my snakes. Seriously, I think you'd better lock my door."

"No," said Pearl. "Let's think positive. You're going to be okay." And if you're not okay, and I need to help you, you wouldn't believe how careful I'll be, she added to herself.

Dusa dumped the pasta into a colander in the sink, then used tongs to lift big portions onto two white china plates, topping both servings with lots of sauce. Her mother added lettuce and ranch dressing. They both moved quickly, with glances at the clock. Tonight there was no question of eating at the table. They picked up their trays and headed through the swing door into the tiny living room. Setting their trays down on side tables at opposite ends of an overstuffed chesterfield covered in a faded floral print, Dusa and her mom sank down comfortably side by side.

For the moment, it was just as if the snakes, the nightmares, the seizures, the attacks and the hospital stay had never happened at all.

Pearl sighed and reached for the remote. Sometimes she felt guilty about eating dinner here, but Dusa was right, it was easier. She was never up to much dinnertime chat, always wiped out after her day in the law office of Sanderson and Jaffey. Later, her energy typically revived, but by then Dusa would be deep in homework or gabbing on the phone with her friends. "Discovery Channel, right?" she asked.

"Right," said Dusa, forking a mouthful of spaghetti. "I'm not getting my hopes up," she said defiantly. In spite of herself, however, she felt the adrenaline surge.

It was an interview show. Onscreen, a man introduced two women, Dr. Teno Gordon, a medical doctor, and Dr. Yali Gordon, a psychologist. Dr. Teno looked squat and dumpy, older than her sister, dark and slightly mustached. In a no-nonsense navy suit, she sat square to the camera. Someone had used a brilliant crimson lipstick on her lips. Dr. Yali, tall, slim and gorgeous in a jungle-print designer pantsuit, looked more like a model than a psychologist. Dusa goggled for a minute before turning her eyes to the middle-aged host. What was his name? She frowned. She didn't like the way he treated people, Mr. Nasty and Nice. Usually she didn't watch him.

"We invited three different neurologists and two well-respected psychologists to join you on the program tonight," Mr. Nasty began. "I have to tell you, ladies, all five of them turned us down flat. 'They may be sincere practitioners,' one of the good doctors told me, 'but I doubt it. I think they've made up the disease they pretend to cure, and I won't be seen with them on your show or in any other public forum.' Strong words, aren't they? Does everybody in the medical establishment think you are charlatans? Are you charlatans?"

"We are not charlatans." Dr. Teno's voice was coldly indignant. "When something is different, out front, little people try to knock it down. It is the nature of an establishment to be suspicious of anything that is outside the common experience. We are outside the common experience. Naturally, the medical establishment frowns on our work and puts obstacles in our way. It is to be expected. You have seen our credentials. We can spend our time arguing about them if you insist."

The interviewer leaned forward. "Snake dreamers," he snarled. "You cure snake dreamers! I've heard of some very strange diseases, but I've never heard of this one, nor have the doctors who head up the Medical Association."

Dusa stopped chewing. Her fork slipped out of her hand and clattered on her plate. She did not notice. Her eyes were fixed on the television screen.

The younger sister laughed, a musical, charming sound. What was her name? Yali, Dr. Yali Gordon; Dusa remembered it easily. Dr. Yali tapped the interviewer's sleeve. Gold bangles jingled on her slim bronzed arm. "Come now," she said lightly, "are you telling me that you—in this business—*you* believe everything the doctors' office tells you?"

The interviewer grinned at her. "It does sound preposterous, all the same," he repeated, "but preposterous can be fascinating. So, tell me, tell our viewers all about your snake dreamers." Enter Mr. Nice, thought Dusa in disgust.

The camera, which had framed the three people around the table, now zoomed in on the fair woman's face. It was a rather angular face, with high cheekbones, a sharp chin and a beaky nose somehow composing a very attractive whole.

Dusa's foot began a rhythmic tapping on the floor. Pearl gave her a startled glance. Her right hand caught Dusa's tray as it began to slide off the girl's lap. Pearl fielded her own tray onto her side table and put Dusa's dinner on the floor; her daughter's eyes never wavered from the woman on the screen.

"The condition is extremely rare," said Dr. Yali, jingling her bangles at the unseen audience, "but not so rare as we first imagined. Now that my sister and I have identified it, patients come, in desperate need of help, so many that we have restricted our practice to treating them."

"In fact, you are good angels," bantered the interviewer.

"Our patients think we are."

"They are all young people, didn't you tell me?" said the interviewer.

"Young women," dumpy Dr. Teno cut in abruptly. The

camera swiveled. Dusa grimaced. Both sisters spoke excellent English, but Dusa was sure the language was not native to them. What, then? She could not even guess.

The interviewer waited, expecting Dr. Teno to continue, but the heavy crimson mouth stayed shut. "How did you get started?" prompted the man. "Have you been treating snake dreamers for a long time?"

The two women looked at each other. A twisted half smile passed between them. "A long time?" echoed dark Dr. Teno. "Oh yes, sometimes it seems like centuries." She gave a deprecating shrug.

"Once there were three of us. We had a younger sister," said Dr. Yali. "We first encountered this condition in relation to her. For longer than you would credit, our dearest wish was to make our sister whole."

"You couldn't help her?"

Both sisters shook their heads, apparently unable to speak. There were tears in Dr. Yali's golden eyes. "Because of what we learned, we have been able to help many others," Dr. Teno said. "We have always dealt with adolescent sleep disorders," she added firmly. "Now we are more specialized, that's all." She locked eyes with the TV host.

"How does the illness begin?" he asked. "Or should I say, the condition?"

"It begins at menarche," replied Dr. Teno. "Overnight, as you might say." Again she closed her mouth.

Dr. Yali added softly, "Call it an illness, call it a condition, what matter? Night after night, their sleep is restless and their dreams are full of serpents. Like the snakes, the sufferers writhe and twist."

Dusa retched, fighting off nausea. Her mother moved close, so that their bodies touched. She put an arm around her daughter's rigid shoulder.

"As bad as that? Why hasn't anybody heard about it, if it's as bad as that?" Mr. Nice sounded shocked.

"Often the young people suffer for many years but do not tell their parents," soft-voiced Dr. Yali replied. "In the early stages, they may try to tell, but no one takes them seriously. In early days, they themselves keep hoping that it will go away as suddenly as it arrived. For a long time they may seem quite normal, but it's all pretense. They learn to fight off sleep, because they are afraid of it, and rightly so. For them, sleep gives no rest, only the snakes."

Pearl's arm tightened.

"After a few years, the victims are thin and harried. Sometimes they are wrongly diagnosed as epileptic, but medication for this condition makes them much worse. When at last they come to us, our patients blame themselves. They are horrified, because now others know their shameful secret." The slim woman shook her head in pity.

The trembling began in Dusa's hands and arms, but in no time her whole body was shaking. Her face was chalk white. Pearl's free hand moved to cover her daughter's fingers. How cold they felt!

"You see, the snake dreamers are convinced that they are different from everybody else. Like all young people, their greatest need is to be accepted and to be part of the crowd. In a vain parody of normalcy, they hide their nightmares and long for them to disappear. Perhaps only the bravest of the sufferers, or the most desperate, convince a parent, or, once in a long while, a much-loved friend."

"Omigod," breathed Dusa. Was it an exclamation or a prayer?

"Oh, Dusa," said Pearl.

Dusa shivered and sobbed and kept her eyes on the screen.

"Hush, darling," said her mother, her voice almost breaking. "Hush then, hush."

In front of them but wholly unaware, the television voices talked about snake dreamers, how other people, doctors and psychologists included, did not understand the violence of their nightmares, the exhausted desperation of their waking hours. Slowly Dusa's trembling subsided and her mother's grip relaxed.

"That's what it's like for you," said Pearl at last, flatly. She felt Dusa nod. "Oh, darling, I wish I'd been able to understand."

"You tried," mumbled Dusa. "You did better than Dr. Andrews."

"Does it still sound preposterous?" asked the slim woman on the screen. "Are we angels or charlatans? What do you think?"

The interviewer shook his head. "What happens when they don't get help?" he asked.

"We are convinced that they often die in early stages. Friends and relatives have come to us, sometimes years later, when they have heard of our work. It's not always suicide, or not obviously so. The snake dreamers are so tired, it must be easy to put a foot wrong and fall, or to drive a car off the road. An illness that might otherwise be minor could carry them off. If they survive, catatonia. It does not come quickly, but it almost always comes. Stupor and extreme rigidity of the limbs are the major physical manifestations.

"We have talked to two women who survived into their twenties without help. Their catatonic phase had been atypical and brief. As they grew older, the nightmares had finally faded, though they had not totally disappeared. Even without our help, those two might have created some semblance of a normal life."

"And with your treatment, Dr. Gordon?"

"Our recovery rate is better than ninety percent with a maximum of three years' treatment," said the older sister. "We define recovery as being free of the mental symptoms, snake dreams and other hallucinations, and the physical ones, uncontrolled muscular spasm, followed by rigidity, for at least a year. We monitor our patients into their twenties. However, in our experience, the condition, once successfully treated, does not recur."

"That means treatment at your clinic in Greece?"

"Correct." The woman continued, "A patient need not live year-round at the clinic, however. She may come for a month or two at a time."

"Sounds expensive," commented the interviewer, his tone halfway between Mr. Nasty and Mr. Nice. Dusa's mother nodded; that was exactly what she had been thinking.

"We can cope," she said to Dusa. "If you need treatment, love, then treatment you shall have." Dusa managed a shaky laugh.

12

"You are here for a conference," said the interviewer. "Some people must have some confidence, or at least some interest, in your work."

"A conference of psychologists," Dr. Teno pointed out. "My sister's colleagues are ready to hear about our work with snake dreamers. Most medical people are not ready yet. If we had not previously established a reputation for impeccable research, we might have been dismissed altogether." She lifted her head and looked directly into the camera. "We will address members of the International Psychological Association tomorrow afternoon. Later, my sister, Dr. Yali Gordon, will appear on a panel with other specialists in rare disorders of adolescents. We would not be invited speakers, believe me, if our colleagues believed us to be charlatans."

"We are not accepting new patients at present," Dr. Yali added quickly. "We *are* looking for one or two special candidates who would agree to be subjects for our research."

Dusa drew a ragged breath. Her mother's attention focused even more deeply on the speaker.

"These young women would have to be in serious need of help. They would also have to waive many of a normal patient's rights. They, and their parents and guardians, would have to put themselves unreservedly in our hands. Our treatment *is* effective." The golden eyes burned into Dusa's mesmerized gaze. "Dozens, hundreds of patients will attest to it. Some doctors, however, sneer at our evidence. 'Anecdotal,' they say.

"We intend to convince the unbelievers. This means that our research subjects must be isolated. As far as possible, every element except our treatment must be kept from affecting them. Further, they must give permission for us to make unusually complete records and to publicize our findings. Eventually, we hope to make our diagnostic strategies and tools of treatment available to other doctors and therapists. We want them to have no doubts about what works and what does not."

"Sometimes an illness is thought to be rare because few doctors know enough to diagnose it, let alone to treat it." The words dropped ponderously from Dr. Teno's crimson mouth. "My sister and I now suspect that this illness may not be as rare as our previous estimates." Dr. Teno leaned forward earnestly. The TV camera zoomed in on her heavy face. "If fearful serpents haunt your dreams, or have done so in the past," she urged, "telephone us. Make your information part of our records. We can help you, even if we cannot accept you for treatment in our clinic; and you will be helping other victims, now and in times to come."

The interview ended with telephone numbers where a message could be left, and a short statement about the conference due to begin the following day, where Dr. Teno Gordon and Dr. Yali Gordon from Greece would speak on snake dreamers, identification and treatment. The interviewer's voice faded into the noisy roar of a commercial extolling the glories of somebody's latest pickup truck.

Pearl wrote down the information; then she found the remote and pressed the Off switch. Automatically her hands went on stroking Dusa's shoulders.

"We can't afford it," said Dusa at last. "Greece! It's too expensive, even if they would take me. Anyway, they're only looking for one person. Two at the most. I haven't got a chance."

"Maybe," said her mother lightly. "Let me look into it, but we won't hold our breath. Okay?"

Dusa laughed. "I won't start packing yet," she answered, just as lightly.

Mother and daughter hugged each other extra hard that night, and Pearl left Dusa's bedroom door wide open. Dusa marveled as she felt herself sink into a snakeless sleep.

Next day, as soon as Dusa had left for school, her mother phoned the television station and left a message for the Gordon sisters—an odd name, that, for two Greek women! When she hung up, she was not at all sure that the receptionist had got her name or phone number right; still less was she convinced that the message would reach its destination. For a minute or two she hesitated, then made a second call to say she would, once again, not be in to work that morning.

At the convention center, men and women with badges rushed about the huge foyer or talked to each other over coffee and muffins. Pearl joined the registration lineup. A woman moved down the line, handing out forms.

Pearl's steps faltered as she scanned the page. "Registration is restricted to health-care professionals," it stated. What could she do about that? She dug frantically in her purse. At last she found the card: Mary Whitehead, Ph.D., Registered Psychologist. Dr. Whitehead had been called in after Dusa's grades had plummeted and her attention span had dropped to preschool levels. Pearl had been shocked when the psychologist asked her where Dusa was getting her drugs and how she was paying for them! Luckily she still had the woman's card; she had intended to tear it into bits and stamp on them. A moment later she picked up her precious badge.

The conference room was hot and airless. Pearl squeezed into a space against the back wall. She could not hear either speaker well, and this talk, unlike the television interview, was very technical. The slim sister, Dr. Yali, wore a black silk pantsuit today, still stunning; the squat, square one, Dr. Teno Gordon, was again wearing the navy serge suit and dark tie. No doubt today's white shirt was fresh, as was the lipstick, bright as blood.

"These slides show various stages, from diagnosis to recovery," said Teno. "This is an extreme case. We'll call her Sara; that is not her name."

Pearl slumped against the wall. As she looked at the image on the screen, bile rose in her throat. "Anorexia," she would have said, and so had Sara's doctors, as Dr. Teno pointed out.

Sara didn't eat, couldn't sleep, but it was because of the snakes: a quick succession of slides gave a movie impression of the bony body writhing on its bed. Three months later, there was some flesh on the skeleton; in six months, the figure looked human; in a year, Sara, in a sweater, showed a modest bust. It was two years before she managed a nervous smile. The end of three years showed a beautiful young woman, confident and calm. With tutoring, Sara was catching up on her studies; she would graduate from high school just one semester behind her class.

Pearl started to push her way toward the speakers before the lights came up. "Five more minutes," called somebody, "then we must clear the room." Pearl had scribbled a note about Dusa. She shoved her way to Yali's side. "It's my daughter," she said, holding out her note. "I beg you, Dr. Gordon, we must speak to you. My Dusa." Pearl's gray eyes filled with tears.

Yali looked up sharply. Bangles clanked and tinkled on her slim arm as she reached for the paper. She held Pearl's eye and nodded as she put the note into her attaché case. "Dusa," she murmured. "Dusa. I will call you this evening, Dr. Whitehead, you can be sure of that."

"But—but—" spluttered Pearl, and then, "It's all in the note, Dr. Gordon. Thank you, thank you from my heart." Her feet moved automatically. She felt wind on her face and realized she was outside. With only a little more awareness, she found herself at the office. The afternoon passed in a blur. When she caught herself putting the Carstairs will in the Folkestone file, Pearl pleaded headache and went home. She and Dusa heated fish and chips and made salad together.

Hesitantly, Pearl told her daughter what she had done. "Dr. Whitehead! Oh, Mom," Dusa laughed. "I hope they don't report you."

Pearl shrugged. "One thing led to another," she said.

They had hardly finished dinner when the doorbell rang. "One of your friends?" asked her mother, but Dusa shook her head. Pearl checked the peephole, then opened the door in amazement. The two Dr. Gordons stood on the little front porch. A taxi was turning around in the drive. "We came," said square Dr. Teno.

"We wanted to," said slim Dr. Yali, smiling. "Is Dusa at home?"

At first Dusa hung back shyly. She could not believe

that these two important people had come to her house, just like that! Pearl, however, did not hesitate. "How good of you," she said at once, taking Yali's black velvet coat and Teno's navy serge. "Dusa, put on tea for our guests."

In no time the two doctors were settled, Yali in a rose plush tub chair, Teno in a high-backed wooden one, with Pearl and Dusa smiling up at them from the chesterfield.

"When did the dreams begin?" asked Teno.

"When I started my periods," replied Dusa, "just like you said. I thought I was never going to start. All my friends had bosoms and hips—and boyfriends. Not me. Beanpole, that was my nickname. Yuck."

"You were so impatient," said Pearl. "It happened halfway through the year Dusa was fifteen," she continued. "You never saw a happier young woman—or a sorrier one."

"Tell us"—Yali was avid—"about the snakes. Tell us everything!"

In memory, the snakes hissed into Dusa's thoughts: listen, lisssten. Thisss isss the way . . .

Dusa's mouth tightened. Even thinking about the snakes was dangerous. She knew how she had fought them for possession of her mind. When the snake voices began, she would recount facts about herself. Last year's facts: I am Dusa, fifteen years old, a freshman at Winston Park. I made the honor roll last term. On Thursdays I play volleyball. On Tuesdays I swim. My favorite course is auto mechanics. My friends think that's pretty crazy; they sure don't need to know I've got a head full of talking snakes.

This year Dusa was sixteen and a sophomore. She was no longer on the honor roll, though she swam most weeks and still played volleyball. She had wanted to take advanced shop, but the class was full, and she was taking computer science. She had been in hospital twice, and the snakes were winning.

Dusa looked helplessly at Yali. Her best efforts were devoted to pushing the snakes away and trying to keep them from possessing her. If she talked about them, if she even thought about them, wouldn't they take over? Even if she took that risk, where would she start?

"What do your snakes look like, Dusa?" asked Teno. "You can describe them, can't you? Begin with that."

"Tell us, darling," her mother urged.

Dusa drew a deep breath. How could Teno know what she was thinking? But it was a place to start, and the others were there to help. "My snakes," she began dreamily. "They are horrible, and they are beautiful. They give me nightmares, and they won't get out of my head, but they are beautiful. There's a big one that's pure gold, with emerald eyes and a forked ruby tongue.

"I never see their tails. That's strange, isn't it, as if all their tails were tied together, like some weird bunch of flowers. Sometimes they're so noisy I can't hear anything else; they all seem to be writhing and hissing. Other times, almost all of them seem to be asleep, but one or two are always moving, looking around. The little snakes are thin as a pencil and only a few inches long. The biggest ones are a couple of feet long or more, nearly as thick as my wrist." Dusa held out her small wrist and stared at it.

"They sound marvelous," sighed Yali.

Dusa shook her head angrily. "I hate them. I'm scared of them. When they are frightened, I can't sleep or eat.

When they are angry, I have fits, and then I can't even move, or else I hit somebody." She looked at her mother. "The doctors say it isn't epilepsy, or not typical epilepsy, but they don't know what it is. The snakes seem to want something from me, and I don't know what they want." She shuddered. "Sounds crazy, doesn't it?"

What would Pearl say, what would the doctors say, if she told them the other part? Sometimes it was as if the snakes were talking to her, in a strange language. Sometimes Dusa fancied she had only to listen more closely and she would understand every word. That was really crazy, and Dusa had, from the very first, made up her mind to say nothing about it.

Pearl said quietly, "Dr. Andrews doesn't think you're crazy, Dusa."

Dusa shrugged and rolled her eyes. What did Dr. Andrews know?

Pearl spoke to the two sisters. "Often I come into Dusa's bedroom and hold her while she screams and writhes." Absently her hand stroked the bruise on her chin. "Sometimes I can't wake Dusa out of the nightmare, not for hours, and her muscles go hard and rigid. She looks as if she is screaming, but she doesn't make a sound. Other times she doesn't wake me, but in the morning I can see she hasn't slept. I started making notes a couple of months ago, when the attacks came, how long they lasted, all the details I could remember."

Dusa shot her a look. "You never told me," she said.

"I couldn't. It was easy to see you were getting worse. Making notes was something to do, and I needed something to do. I hoped it would be useful sometime." Pearl turned back to Yali and Teno.

"Did you write up your notes?" asked Teno.

"How very intelligent of you," chimed in Yali. "How soon can we see your report?"

For the first time in months, it seemed, the muscles in Pearl's neck and shoulders relaxed. She ran upstairs, returning with two stapled copies. "I gave a copy to Dr. Andrews before Dusa went into hospital," she continued, handing one lot of pages to Teno and the other to Yali, "but I'm not sure he read it. Dusa doesn't look as bad as that girl you showed on the screen, but she is certainly getting worse. Is that where she is heading?"

"Give us a few minutes to read," Yali replied. "Then we can give you a better answer." For the following quarter of an hour, Yali and Teno read and reread Pearl's report. Teno made notes. Yali read through quickly, then began paging back and forth, nodding now and again.

"I feel like an insect on a pin," Dusa muttered irritably.

"I know," Pearl whispered.

At last Teno looked up. As soon as she began to speak, Yali too raised her eyes. "You ask where Dusa is heading," said Teno evenly. "Your notes make it very clear, Pearl. I don't know that I've ever seen such thoughtful observation from somebody who is not a trained professional. This is not a mild case. If it is not treated, periods of catatonia will develop, then get longer, with less respite. Before she is twenty, Dusa will be unable to speak, to hear, to see, or to move. Her body will become rigid. You will have a stone maiden for your child. It would be a tragedy."

Dusa shivered. Already she felt the chill of that stony condition. She was right beside her mother, as close as if they were joined at the hip, but no warmth from the older woman's body transferred itself to the younger one.

"Dusa," Yali asked softly, "do you truly want to be rid of the snakes? We will have to explore your feelings about them. They are beautiful, you are right. You are scared and angry; so are they. Is part of you drawn to them? I think so. Your cure will be difficult. They won't want to go, and you don't altogether want it either." For a moment, her golden eyes seemed to bore into Dusa's very soul.

"Can you cure her?" asked Pearl. "Can you do it for sure? Is Dusa a good subject for your research?"

"In any serious illness," responded Teno, "there are no guarantees. I'm sure you know that. I suggest that Yali and I do an assessment. We'll need in-depth interviews with Dusa, and with you, Pearl, as well as some tests and a review of Dusa's medical records. I'd like your permission to consult with her doctor. Dr. Andrews, is that his name?"

"There are many decisions to be made," added Yali. "If we accept you for our research project, Dusa, it must be on the terms we outlined. Don't expect it to be easy. You would have to work with us when you're tired, when you're angry, when you want to give up and go home, even when you're ill. You would be away from your mother, likely for several months. Sometimes you'll be convinced that we're your enemies, though nothing could be further from the truth. How would you feel about all that?"

Dusa's eyes were enormous. She yawned suddenly. "I

22

don't know," she said. "I hated being away from Mom in the hospital, but I can't go on living with the snakes. I don't know. You're scaring me." She looked anxiously at her mother.

"Me too," said Pearl.

Teno nodded. "Good," she said. "This is a very serious commitment. Why don't you talk it over? Write down your questions, I'm sure you'll have lots of them. We'll tell you what we can. For one thing, you need to know more about us."

Before last night, Pearl had never heard of the two Dr. Gordons. Before tonight, she had never met them. Pearl shivered. She had felt ready to push her daughter out the door, to give her precious child into the hands of strangers. "You're right," she agreed.

"On the other hand," Yali added firmly, "you mustn't be discouraged. This could work out well for all of us. Teno, do you agree?"

"Yali and I do not always see things the same way," said Teno cheerfully, "but I agree with her about this. You're nervous, Dusa." Teno's dark eyes, fixed on Dusa, seemed suddenly to penetrate to her very core. "That's not surprising. We won't rush you. Whatever comes of this, you must feel right about it."

"You stole my line." Yali nodded.

Dusa could feel the serpents stirring in her head, could hear the little hisses that signaled another snake-possessed night. Her frightened glance fixed on Teno, then swung to Yali. "You *can* help me, can't you?" she cried.

Both sisters sat absolutely still, dark eyes and golden deep and kind. Although neither said a word, Dusa felt the snakes subsiding, the little hisses fading, and calmness entering her soul. Yali spoke at last. "Be comforted, child. We can help you, and we surely will."

"Don't go," Dusa urged, and then the absurdity of it overcame her, these two strangers in her own living room, and that sudden impulse she had felt to run to them and hang on for dear life. She laughed shakily and clutched her mother's hand.

"Let me give you Dr. Andrews's card," said Pearl to Teno and Yali. "I'll phone him in the morning and tell him to expect your call." Inside Dusa's head, the last vestige of her snake world subsided.

Teno tucked the card into a side pocket in her big leather bag and dug out her own card, and Yali's, for Pearl. "Check us out with our professional organizations," she said. "You'll find we are members in good standing. I did my medical training in Greece, so you'll have to take that on faith, but Yali has a degree in psychology from Northwestern University in Illinois. The present head of department was her faculty advisor. I'll give you his telephone number." She grinned at her sister. "With any luck, Pearl will hear all the wild stories of your misspent youth."

Yali chuckled. "Better my misspent youth than yours, sister dear," she said lightly. "Don't scare Pearl or Dusa, if you please."

Thank goodness, thought Pearl, relieved by the bit of teasing. They are human. Dusa will have a chance to laugh.

Yali nodded, almost as if she had read the thought. "I brought brochures about our clinic. This is where you will stay, Dusa, if it all works out." She handed one glossy

24

folder to Dusa, the other to Pearl. "Don't try to look at it tonight," she added gently. "Morning is time enough.

"Can we get together for some testing tomorrow, Dusa?" she added. "Early afternoon, perhaps?" Plans were quickly made and a taxi summoned to take the Gordons back to their hotel. It was easy after all for Dusa, arm in arm with her mother in the little front hall, to see them leave. Tomorrow would indeed be time enough.

CHAPTER 2

Dusa's door was open again that night, and the threatened nightmares did not materialize. For a second blessed night, her dreams were free of snakes. Over breakfast she and Pearl picked up the brochures.

The front page was dominated by a color photo of the Gordon Clinic. Under the photo was an Athens address, as well as telephone and fax numbers. "Isn't it amazing!" exclaimed Dusa. She smiled in incredulous delight. She and Pearl were gazing at a miniature castle, a two-story structure finished in white stucco. At each end of the building, a conical tower lifted one more story. Between the towers, the roof was flat and balustraded. The exquisite building perched on top of a cliff. Terraced gardens hugged the foundation. Below the gardens, a long gray staircase zigzagged down the cliff to the slaty sea where a launch was tied up to some kind of pier. From wherever the photo had been taken, the launch looked like a toy.

"It's really something," Pearl agreed. The inside two

pages of the folded brochure described the program at the clinic, which could accommodate up to twelve patients and eight staff.

"Look!" Dusa pointed to a section headed, "Recreation."

" 'Swimming and boating are regular activities, supervised by qualified staff. Special opportunities may be offered to study the archaeology of ancient Greece.' Oh, Mom, I want to go." The section was followed by a list giving names and qualifications of Yali and Teno and other staff members, two psychologists, a physiotherapist and a nurse.

The back page gave prices, along with a tear-off inquiry form. Dusa took one horrified look. "We can't afford it," she said flatly. Her heart sank. Dusa had always thought it a ridiculous image, ocean waves swamping a red satin heart. Now it was visceral, and not ridiculous at all.

Pearl studied the back page of her own brochure. "You're right. From what they say about how long the treatment takes, we can't afford it, not even if I sold the house. This brochure is for regular patients, though, not research subjects. Yali and Teno know that we're not rich. Maybe we don't have to pay these rates."

It was the first question Dusa asked when she met the sisters in their hotel suite that afternoon. "Do we have to pay what it says in the brochure? If we do, you don't need to bother interviewing me."

Yali frowned. "That was stupid of me. I should have crossed out the prices, or told you they did not apply. Sit down and relax, if you please." Dusa perched on the edge of a dark green armchair.

"Dusa, I gave you the brochure for background information, and for the pictures. Our island home is very beautiful. I hoped you might imagine yourself living there, in a tower room perhaps." She shook her head.

"Usually a research subject receives pay," said Teno. "University students often earn extra money that way. We'll have to talk to your mother about this, Dusa, and we must remember that nothing is settled yet. Perhaps you are not the person we are looking for. Perhaps you will decide, for whatever reasons, not to accept our offer, if we make one. We might pay our subject a small amount, or we might subsidize that person's transportation to Athens instead." Her eyes blazed, and her voice suddenly rang out, "If we choose you, and you choose us, believe me, money will not be a problem."

I wouldn't want to get in *your* way, thought Dusa, as Teno's scarlet lips clamped shut. Power radiated from the dumpy body in the navy suit. Against that power, Dusa felt certain, even the snakes would shrink and wriggle away. "I'm glad," she said. "I'm *very* glad. Let's get on with it, then. What do you want to know?" Teno might say that nothing was settled yet, but already Dusa could see herself looking out at the ocean from the windows of a white tower somewhere in Greece.

Teno's square crimson lips curved into a stiff smile. "Are you comfortable?" Dusa pushed herself back in the oversized chair. Both Teno and Yali picked up notebook and pen.

"For the record, please state your name," Teno began the interview.

"Dusa Thrasman," replied the girl, smiling.

"Your full name."

"That is my full name. I don't have a middle name."

"Your first name, Medusa. Medusa, isn't it." Teno did not put it as a question.

"No," said Dusa, flushing. How she hated anybody to try to call her that! "Mom named me Dusa—she was a character in some old play, *Dusa, Fish, Stas and Vi.*"

"Dusa, then." Teno wrote in her book. Have it your own way, her gesture said. "This Dusa, the one you are named for, did she have snaky hair?"

In the chair, Dusa sat bolt upright. Where was her coat?

"Now Teno," said Yali softly, "don't give Dusa a hard time."

"There's a connection," said Teno. "A Medusa connection—there must be! Don't resist it, Dusa."

Suddenly Dusa was terrified. She could feel the snakes stirring. "What connection? *I* don't have snaky hair! *I* don't turn people to stone!"

"Of course not," soothed Yali.

"Of course you don't," Teno instantly agreed. "I am sorry, Dusa. Relax. I did not mean to frighten you." She looked at Yali in silent appeal.

"Sometimes Teno pushes, mostly to see what response she gets. So, now we know you aren't easy to push." Yali smiled. "Are you all right?" she asked.

Dusa's heart was still racing. She looked warily at Teno, who made a wry face, then back at Yali.

Yali waited for Dusa's stiff nod. "Good. Let's go on. Teno had a long talk with Dr. Andrews this morning, and he has given us a copy of your medical record. He has made very full notes of his observations and his attempts to treat you. He is a good doctor, Dusa. He knows nothing of snake dreamers, but he cares about you and wants you to be well. His notes and your mother's report have told us a great deal about your illness. Now we need to hear from you. Is there one episode that stands out in your mind?"

Dusa's knuckles whitened on the arms of the big chair.

"I see," said Yali softly. "Tell us about that one."

Dusa's head moved automatically, pushing frantically against the smothering folds of the stinking bag. She was losing herself; the horror was happening again.

Where were her arms? Where were her legs? She had no sense of any part of her body, only of her head, which rolled and jerked in the grasp of some unseen hand. Slimy leather pressed against her face; she knew the bag that held her was made of leather, rotting leather soaked in blood. Her mouth and eyes were closed tight. How she wished she could close her nostrils!

All around her in the stinking bag, the snakes pushed too. They seemed to be part of her, those snakes, jerking her head as they moved, sharing her terror and rage; and that connection was horrible, worse perhaps than the blackness, worse than the stench of decay. In her nightmare there was no light at all, yet Dusa knew each snake, the blue and gold stripes on this one, the black diamonds on that. Each snake had a name, and in the dream she could have called each one by name, and it would have answered her with a loving hiss. A loving hiss!

Where was she? Who was she? Why was she shut up with the snakes? The dreamer struggled, frantic to escape.

Slowly, bag, snakes and smell faded. Dusa looked down curiously at the dark green leather chair, then around her at the mahogany and brass of the room. A glass-topped table. Her forehead was cold. Yali knelt by her side on the dark red carpet, stroking her arm. Teno breathed heavily. They knew, Dusa was certain. How could they know? Had she talked in her dream? It was a comfort, knowing that they knew. Dusa could not lift an arm, could not push herself to her feet, could barely lift an eyelid right then, might never lift an eyelid again.

"Brave girl," said Teno, in a husky voice. Were there tears in Dr. Teno's eyes? How strange!

"Bring us a blanket, would you, Teno," said Yali, still patting Dusa's arm. "How about some hot tea? Cookies too, or cake. Something sweet."

Teno bustled about, and soon Dusa was getting warm again, wrapped in a four-striped Hudson's Bay blanket, sipping hot, sweet tea.

"Better?" asked Yali gently.

Dusa nodded.

"Can we try one more question? It is not about your snakes, I promise you." She hesitated, appraising the pale cheeks and dull eyes of the girl in the chair.

At last Dusa nodded again, and Yali continued, "What do you know of your own ancestry? Let me tell you why I ask. We believe there is a genetic component in your condition. The snake dreamer's gene may be carried by men or women, though the condition is experienced only by women. The condition, in a mild form, may be experienced every third generation; in every ninth generation, it is severe."

Every ninth generation? "How in the world do you know?" Dusa blurted.

"There are snake dreamers in our family," replied Yali. "You have heard about our sister. She was not the only one. We have good records, and they go a long way back. Now, please tell us what you can about your people."

Dusa did her best. As she talked about her family, her nightmare faded, and her energy began to return. She did not really remember her father. After he died in a car crash, she and her mother had lived with her mom's folks; the little house had belonged to them. Her grandfather's people had emigrated from Ireland a hundred and fifty years ago, "but Grandma was born in Egypt," said Dusa dreamily. "She looked after me all the time before I went to school. She used to tell me stories. I don't remember them much."

"Ah," said Yali softly. "Perhaps some of those stories were about snakes."

"No," said Dusa violently, but in her head Grandma sat beside her once again, and bits of Grandma's stories began to echo in her mind, stories about Grandma's Egyptian great-great-great-great grandmother who dressed in long gauzy skirts and danced, with gold around her neck, gold dripping from her ears, and serpents twined around her arms.

"Hypnosis, do you think?" murmured Teno. "She is an excellent subject."

"At the clinic, we could help you remember nine generations back," said Yali, with glittering eyes. "More than two hundred years!"

"I don't want to," said Dusa vehemently. "Two hundred years, two hundred and fifty, whatever, and I'm 'remembering' a crazy Egyptian dancer with bracelets that hiss. No, thank you very much."

Yali and Teno exchanged quick looks. "That's not a long time for an oak tree," Teno mused, "but for a mayfly, even a highly intelligent mayfly, it would be beyond imagining. Time is not an absolute quantity; it's all in the point of view. With our help, you can recover your grandmother's stories, Dusa, her stories, and her mother's, and her mother's mother's, nine generations back, and then another nine. Don't you know what you just said, Dusa, 'a dancer with bracelets that hiss'?"

Dusa shivered.

"Maybe it doesn't mean anything," said Yali. "We won't take you places that either you or we don't need to go; and, Dusa, if you don't need to go, I don't expect we would either. We know there are stories on your mother's side of your family, that's good enough for now. What about your father's people?"

Dusa shrugged angrily. "It's an English name," she said, "but that's about as much as I know. My dad's dad was killed in World War II when he was a baby, and his mom brought him to Canada. She died before I was born."

"We'll ask your mom," said Yali, "but you may know more than she does, even if you don't realize it. Some memories are carried in your genes."

"Why bother?" Dusa was bewildered. "I'm not my grandparents. I'm me."

"It could help the project," said Teno eagerly. "You

have such empathy, Dusa; there must be a history of snake dreamers in your family. You could be the key to our big breakthrough."

"She's right, Dusa," put in Yali. "I can't tell you how important this is." She made a face, as if to make fun of her own intensity. "Of course, we have our own personal connection."

"Your sister," Dusa murmured.

"Our sister," Teno agreed. "Her time is coming, I know it. She will have her revenge."

"Revenge?" Now Dusa was thoroughly confused. "I thought you couldn't help her. I thought," she hesitated, "I thought she must be dead. What do you mean, revenge?"

"I'm sorry," said Teno smoothly, "my mind was wandering. I meant, you'll have your revenge on people like that school psychologist your mom told us about, you know, the one who thought you were taking drugs. You are very strong, Dusa. You are living with the snakes and not turning catatonic like the others. I'm deeply glad we came to Toronto and met you."

"I'm pretty sure they want me," said Dusa later. She looked at Pearl across the kitchen table and pushed her half-full dinner plate away.

"You've got good instincts about people," Mom replied. "I expect you're right. Dr. Andrews is highly impressed. The two Dr. Gordons are well known internationally, it seems, and have been for more than thirty years. They gave Dr. Andrews a list of their publications, and he picked out three entries and looked them up: the first one on the list, one from the middle, and a recent one."

"Tricky! I guess they checked out okay."

"Sure did. All the articles were published in medical or psychological journals. One was in German, but the other two were in English, and the library faxed copies to him. 'Very thorough,' he said. 'Those two must have been doing research while they were still at university, and started publishing the minute they got their degrees. Even at that, they must be older than they look.'

" 'Would you let them treat your daughter?' I asked him.

" 'I would in a minute, if she was sick like Dusa,' he told me. He didn't miss a beat. 'I want to know what's wrong with her, and I want her to be one hundred percent cured, and they're the best chance I've seen. If they offer to treat Dusa, for heaven's sake jump at it.'

" 'Even if she has to go to Greece and I can't go with her?'

" 'Ouch!' he said. 'I don't like that. But yes, even then.' That's our good doctor's opinion. You think they want you, Dusa. How do you feel about them?"

"I like Yali a lot," said Dusa, "but Teno can be a bit weird. I think Dr. Andrews is right, though. They're not just the best chance, they're the only chance I've seen. Mom, I keep thinking: What if I was like stone, the way they say, and the snakes were living full-time in my head? What if I was there in my head, Mom, along with the snakes? Oh, Mom, I'm so scared."

Pearl squeezed her daughter until Dusa said, "Ease off, Mom. You'll break a rib. If I go to Greece, we can talk on the phone. I'm not dropping off the face of the earth. There'll be other girls as well, snake dreamers like me, and boating, and swimming, and archaeology. And they haven't asked me yet."

"I want to do more checking," said Pearl, "maybe talk to somebody they've treated, somebody they've cured, and her parents too."

"You sound as if you don't trust them," said Dusa, drawing back. "Don't put them off me. I trust them, and I'm the one who's going. If they ask."

Pearl compromised by asking Dr. Andrews to get names and telephone numbers. "Former patients and their parents," said Dr. Andrews. "Nothing wrong with the idea. I thought of it myself, but then I thought how I'd feel if someone asked to talk to former patients of mine. It's tricky. The former patient and the parents would have to be asked, and would have to agree. It's stressful, talking to strangers about such private matters. The Gordons may not want to put anybody through it."

"Will you ask them?" said Pearl quietly. "If you won't, I will."

The Gordons, asked, were sweetly reasonable, pointing out all the difficulties Dr. Andrews had foreseen, plus one he had not considered. "If we were in our office," said Teno, "this would be much easier. Certainly there are people we could approach, people who have already offered. We'll have to think who might be suitable and phone our office to check their files for current information. You'd want an English speaker, of course. Leave it with us, Dr. Andrews, but please understand that it may take a day or two. Hmm, what time is it in Hong Kong?"

A day went by. Pearl, wishing she had closer relatives and more of them, phoned her cousin in Boston. "*Greek* doctors?" said Charlene. "Pearl, I can't believe you wouldn't do better here in the U.S.A."

Pearl tried to explain, but it was a most unsatisfactory conversation.

"I don't know why you called me," Charlene said at last. "You aren't listening to a thing I say."

Amen to that, Pearl thought, glad after all that her nearest relative was almost a thousand miles away. She started to dial Elizabeth's number, but put the phone back in the cradle before it could ring in her friend's apartment. Elizabeth would listen, but Pearl would have to listen to Elizabeth afterward, and Elizabeth could one-up somebody else's problem every time.

Dusa fretted. "Phone somebody," Pearl suggested. "Get your mind off it." But Dusa was too dejected to pick up the phone.

"The Gordons don't want me after all," she said. "Why would they? I'm such a mess."

Pearl fought and conquered a strong inclination to shake her child. They went to bed, but neither of them fell asleep. In Dusa's head the snakes stirred. At last the girl's eyes closed. Almost at once, the nightmares began. Pearl heard Dusa thrashing about, heard the little nonsense grunts, and knew that Dusa was screaming in her sleep but could not make anybody hear. This might be a seizure, one of the bad attacks that looked like epilepsy but apparently was not. Pearl ran into the room. Dusa's lips were already blue, her body rigid, her back arched. Pearl turned Dusa on her side. Her body turned all in a piece.

Rigor mortis, thought Pearl. This is how Dusa's body would feel if she was dead. Hysterical laughter bubbled up, and Pearl fought it. Dusa is not dead, she told herself. I need something so she can't accidentally bite her tongue.

There was no washcloth in sight. Pearl was not about to run to the bathroom to get one. Dusa had put her clothes away, except for a T-shirt draped over her chair. Pearl rolled a bit of shirt and stuck the roll between Dusa's teeth. Then she sat down to watch. The minutes crawled by. After what seemed like an hour, but was likely no more than ten minutes, Dusa began to stir.

Tears of exhaustion, despair and relief dripped down Pearl's cheeks. What would happen if Dusa had a seizure like this when she was home alone? Pearl held Dusa, ignoring any possibility of danger from her child, and they fell asleep in each other's arms. Afterward, Dusa did not talk about the episode, which meant either that she was not aware of it or that she had chosen to say nothing.

Morning brought good news. Dr. Andrews had telephone numbers for Alison and her parents in Sydney and Debbie and her father in San Francisco. Alison and her parents would talk to Pearl; Debbie's father would talk to Dr. Andrews. Debbie herself was studying for exams and not available. "I'll call the minute I've any news," Dr. Andrews promised.

Pearl had hardly hung up the phone when the Gordons called, asking her to meet them that evening at their hotel. Pearl, still tired and worried, agreed. Dusa's treatment could not be delayed. Surely she or Dr. Andrews would reach one family or the other sometime during the day. However, 1 P.M. in Toronto was, it turned out, 4 A.M. in Sydney. Pearl quickly calculated that 6 P.M. Toronto time was the earliest she could reasonably telephone Alison's family. By then, Dusa would be home. Pearl's fingers drummed anxiously on her desk. She would not have time for much of a conversation with the Australians, even without the prospect of making explanations to Dusa as well. Why hadn't she told Dusa about her inquiries? She had thought it would be better if she did her research first, that was all.

Dr. Andrews telephoned shortly before noon. According to Debbie's father, the Gordon sisters walked on water. Debbie had been flown to their clinic a virtual skeleton. Now a college senior, she was a straight-A student, planning to be married in June. Her father did not want her to be reminded that snakes had once haunted her sleeping and waking hours, but he had no doubt that the Gordons had saved her life.

At dinnertime, as soon as Dusa took her tray into the living room, Pearl picked up the phone. While it rang in Sydney, she mentally rehearsed opening lines to Alison's mother or father, or to Alison herself, hoping at the same time that Dusa would not come out to see what her mother was doing. Pearl counted six of the foreign double rings. She didn't really *need* to talk to these people now, after Dr. Andrews's report. They weren't home, that settled it. Pearl hung up. On the whole, she was thankful her call had gone unanswered. She had little enough time to eat dinner and get her thoughts in order before she left for the hotel.

As she expected, Yali and Teno wanted Dusa to go with them.

"I'm truly sorry," said Yali, "that I can't invite you as well. You and Dusa are very close. But if you are there, when Dusa gets better, somebody will be able to say, 'So what did you do? Took a mother and daughter and put them together full-time with expert counseling and therapy for both of them. So the girl is cured of an unusual hysteria. Why not? It's an ideal version of a conventional treatment.' This has been said in the past, Pearl. It's hard for us to argue that a mother's presence makes no difference. In fact, we believe it does make a difference, usually positive, occasionally not. We are certain, however, that our treatment, not the mother's presence, brings about the cure. It will be useful for us to prove it to ourselves, as well as to other doctors."

Pearl sat in silence, watching both sisters intently. Dusa wanted to go with the Gordons. Already Pearl could see her child transferring loyalty and trust to these chance-met strangers. She struggled not to let painful feelings cloud her judgment. She was losing her daughter, Dusa was slipping away. Adolescent rebellion, Pearl thought resentfully, would have been easy to cope with; snake dreams were not. What choice did Dusa have? What choice did her mother have? Hope is preferable to despair.

"It's a generous offer," Pearl said heavily at last. "Thank you. Dusa and I accept."

Now that the decision had been made, the Gordons

wanted to get home as soon as possible. Pearl agreed. The sooner Dusa's treatment began, the better. The sooner Pearl got back to a regular routine at the office, the better. Her boss was a patient man, but Pearl could see all too clearly that his patience was running out.

The next week passed in a frantic blur. Passports (Pearl's, too, so that she could visit), school arrangements, shopping for clothes and various supplies (the Gordons provided a list and some money for the extras), a last visit with Dr. Andrews, tearful partings from school friends; there was hardly time to breathe. Pearl told Dusa about Debbie, and about her plan to talk to Alison; however, she had mislaid Alison's number, and had neither time nor inclination to make a thorough search for it.

The Gordons bought Dusa a ticket to Athens, a one-way ticket, because Dusa might be away for more than a year. Pearl cried when she put down the phone. How she wished Dusa's father were still alive! Was she doing the right thing? Then she dried her tears and went on packing. The Gordons met Pearl and Dusa at the Greek consulate and arranged for Dusa's visa. Already Dusa was sleeping better than she had for many months. The snakes did not disappear from her mind, but they curled there serenely, quiescent and content.

🁢🁢🁢🁢🁢🁢 CHAPTER 3

Dusa was sure she would not sleep on the evening flight; she was much too keyed up. It felt very strange to leave her mother behind—for how long she had no notion—but already her life in Toronto was fading into the past and the new reality taking over.

Dusa occupied the right-hand window seat in the fourth row of the business class cabin of a Boeing 747 bound for Athens. The other passengers were a few men in suits and ties. Most of the oversize seats were empty. Dusa noticed that several men got out computers and files, just like in the TV commercials. They didn't even bother to look out the windows!

The plane rose, circling over the city. There was Highway 401, lighted ribbons of concrete and asphalt enlarged at intervals by intricate knots, the cloverleaf patterns of entrance and exit, small as a model railroad. Looking south, Dusa could see the CN Tower, a skinny needle against the lake, its beacon flashing. Then the lake was spread out gray-black under them. A moment later, they flew into cloud, solid as snow, emerging later to night sky and stars.

Yali sat on Dusa's left, Teno across the aisle. "We can trade around later," Yali said, as calm as if she did this every day.

Likely she does do it often enough, Dusa reminded herself. "I keep wanting to pinch myself," she confided.

"So you'll know it's real?"

Dusa nodded. "It's so amazing," she said. "Lucky me."

"I think it's amazing too," said Yali warmly. "We went to Toronto for a conference presentation, and we're going home with the person we need for our big project. Lucky you, and lucky us." The flight attendant came around with drinks and snacks. "Here's to your cure," Yali toasted her.

"Here's to our project, Dusa, and your cure," Teno added. Dusa raised her glass of diet Coke, smiled, and drank. If only Mom were here, this would be perfect. Dusa pushed the thought away. She had expected to be thrilled, and she was thrilled, but also very sleepy. She was vaguely aware when the attendant took her tray and Yali wrapped a warm blanket around her and slipped a pillow under her head.

Teno and Yali had told her about the flight at Toronto airport, while they waited to board. "We stop in London," Teno had told her, "then we go right through to Athens."

"What happens then?" Dusa had asked.

"Then"—Yali had paused dramatically—"then a cab takes us out to our little Cessna and Teno flies us home. Or I do. We'll be on the island by dinnertime tomorrow."

Dusa had felt her mouth fall open, her blue eyes goggling. "Did Mom know about this?" she'd gasped. "Why didn't she tell me?"

Teno had laughed. "Of course we told your mom," she'd said. "She thought it would be fun for us to tell you ourselves, to let it be our special surprise."

"You can both fly?" Dusa had asked, even though Teno had already said so.

"We can," Yali had replied. "Teno is perhaps a little stronger, but we are both very experienced."

Dusa had given up "amazing" as her response of choice, but no other word came to her. "Amazing," she'd said, with conviction. Wait till she got back to school and told her friends about this! "Is there anything you can't do?" she'd asked.

The moment the words were out of her mouth she'd been sorry. Yali's mouth drooped, and her golden eyes, which had been laughing, had suddenly filled with pain. Teno's square shoulders had slumped.

"Your sister," Dusa had gulped, understanding immediately. She could still feel her cheeks burning. "I'm so sorry," she'd mumbled.

"That's all right," Teno had said evenly. "You can't be watching your every word, Dusa, and we don't want you to try. Don't you worry about us."

Yali had patted Dusa's arm. Remembering, Dusa felt the sting of tears.

"I am sorry, though," she'd said again. Maybe she could steer the conversation to a happier topic. "Tell me about your plane," she'd asked.

Teno had smiled as if she knew perfectly well why Dusa

had asked, but was willing to play along. She'd described the Cessna as a four-seater single-engine float plane, adapted for extra cargo. "A C-180 float," Yali had added.

"The aircraft is not new," Teno had continued, "but we're used to it. It's our hobby—well, one of our hobbies. We do the maintenance ourselves." Dusa had gazed at her wide-eyed.

Now, as Dusa sank deeper into sleep a very strange thought came to her. Perhaps, just perhaps, she would in the end be grateful to the snakes for choosing her.

"This is your captain speaking." The words blared over the intercom, and Dusa woke with a start. She opened her eyes. Yali and Teno were both staring intently down at her. Funny, she hadn't realized it, Yali's eyes were golden and fierce, like the eagle Dusa used to watch at the zoo, only here no cage came in between. "Go to sleep, child," Yali murmured, hooding her eyes, and Dusa drifted off.

The snakes were quiescent as the big plane pushed through the sky. Yali and Teno slept as well. Then Yali moved in her sleep, throwing an arm against Dusa's body. In the girl's head, the snakes went mad, hissing, writhing. It was as if they all emitted some variation, loud or soft, less intense or more so, of the same unbearably shrill note. Dusa jerked awake, screaming. Around her, male voices cursed. Attendants rushed about, soothing and calming.

With strong arms, Yali lifted the terrified girl into her own seat and held her, crooning gently, much as her mother might have done.

Teno signaled the flight attendant to bring a glass of

water. She fished a small vial out of her purse, opened it, and poured out a purple capsule. "Dusa," she said. The voice was kind, but full of authority. "Help her sit up, Yali. Dusa, I want you to take this capsule. It will help you. Take it now, Dusa."

Dusa gulped and swallowed.

Yali eased her down again and patted her shoulder. "That's the girl."

Dusa slept through the stop at Heathrow. She never stirred as the big plane took off again. Yali jiggled her gently when the attendant came around with breakfast. Dusa slept on. "Eight o'clock and all's well," said Yali. "Come on, sleepyhead, rise and shine."

Dusa half opened her eyes, smiled at Yali, and shut them again. Five days ago, she thought dreamily, I'd never seen these two women, and here I am, as if I'd been with them all my life. She ate her breakfast, brushed her teeth, and went back to sleep again.

Yali roused her shortly before they began their approach. "Your first sight of Athens," she said. "It would be a shame to sleep through that!"

Dusa agreed. "I never sleep like that," she said. "I don't know what got into me." Teno shrugged. Dusa obviously had no memory of the purple pill.

Now Yali could not stop talking about all the marvelous sights Dusa was going to see. "We won't be spending all our time at the clinic," she said gaily. "No, no. We'll do the tourist things, Dusa, you must make the pilgrimage up the Acropolis—that's the great eminence where the Parthenon was built, and many other temples. We'll see a drama cycle at the old theater: three plays that tell one long story, and maybe a satyr play afterwards.

"But Dusa, we'll take you places that tourists never go. You shall see the real Greece, child, this ancient land as it has been in times long past, time out of mind, as the folk say hereabouts. Do you know the old stories, Dusa? We'll take you where they happened." Yali's golden eyes burned as she spoke. Around them other people, dark-haired people mostly, chatted and laughed exuberantly, though even the intonation of the language was strange to Dusa. "They're happy to be going home," Yali said softly.

"In the summer, this plane would be all tourists," put in Teno. "Silly people, Athens is too hot for sight-seeing then. Athenians go away. October is a good month here."

"A good month on the island too." Yali smiled cheerfully at a large fair woman with a camera who had turned to look at them from the row ahead.

Compared to Toronto, the airport at Athens was small. The passengers disembarked via a metal platform and steps that had been wheeled up to the plane's door. They walked across hot tarmac to the shelter of a flat, rather grubby building. Athens. After all the hype, it didn't look like much. The two Dr. Gordons and their young patient cleared customs with a speed that Dusa might have found impressive if she had been a more experienced traveler.

"Can we go to the Acropolis today?" Dusa asked, as they followed the skycap and their luggage toward the door.

"We hadn't planned to," said Teno. "They're expecting

us at home. We've been away a week longer than we intended."

"Plans can be changed," Yali said thoughtfully. "We could stay in Athens tonight and go home in the morning."

Dusa blushed again. "I didn't know we'd have to stay overnight," she said. "I know you want to get back to the clinic. I've been thinking about the other girls. Do you miss them? I bet they miss you, a lot. I thought we could just go to the Acropolis for a little while."

"We usually spend all day," said Yali, "and come away wishing we could stay longer. Now that I think of it, though, that's not the best plan for you. The place is overwhelming." She looked at her sister. Dusa sensed some wordless communication between them, before Yali went on talking. "Teno," she said, "we don't want to start Dusa off with a disappointment, do we. We can introduce her to the Parthenon and see some of the marbles in the museum, and still get home for dinner. Teno, what do you say?"

"Let's do it," Teno agreed. The red lips formed a natural, and very agreeable, smile. "Taxi!"

Yali put an arm around Dusa's shoulder as their luggage was loaded into the cab, then they were bowling along green boulevards, Teno chatting with the driver, paying no attention to the slow lament of a singer on the radio. Could it be Nana Mouskouri? Mom's favorite. Dusa shivered. For hours, it seemed, no thought of Mom had crossed her mind. She should have phoned from the airport; she had promised. Now Teno and Yali had changed their plans to give her a treat, and she didn't want the treat anymore, not until she talked to Mom. "Is there a phone at the Acropolis?" she asked.

"A phone?" Teno looked back over the seat, eyebrows raised.

"Oh," said Yali, "to call your mom. We should have phoned from the airport. I thought of it, then we got going on this idea, and it went right out of my mind. I'm sorry, Dusa. There are telephones in the shop at the museum, but it may be difficult to get an overseas connection. We'll try, but it may have to wait." She made a face at her own forgetfulness.

Dusa tried to look around her as they whirled along, but buildings, parks, even a statue that Yali pointed out, were dulled by guilt. On the horizon, clouds were moving in, though the noonday sun still shone warm in a deep blue sky. The taxi halted outside entrance gates at the foot of the high Acropolis hill. "He'll wait with our luggage," said Yali, catching Dusa's anxious look.

Beside the gates, in both directions, vendors squatted with their wares. Dusa hardly noticed them, nor had she really paid attention to the extraordinary buildings above. Her eyes were fixed on the ascent. A man rushed over to them, waving a garish sketch.

"Buy my painting, ladies. I make you the best price."

Teno smiled, and said a few words in Greek. The man laughed good-naturedly and went back to his place.

Ordinarily Dusa would have loved the walk up the hill. The wide zigzag road was full of people, some climbing, others descending. As they climbed, the view became spectacular, but Dusa never paused, even when her breathing became ragged. Teno and Yali kept pace with her easily, exchanging glances now and again.

Dusa passed the exquisite temple of Athene Nike without lifting her eyes, but when they made the next turn, and faced the majesty of the Parthenon, Yali put out a gentle hand. "Dusa," she said, "stop. Look at it. Let this world fade, child, and the cares of this world, and look at it."

The Parthenon. Dusa looked. She breathed deeply, and kept on looking. The great gleaming pillars, the astounding roof stretched before her. She recognized it, of course. She had seen pictures of it, she had seen it on TV. But she had never seen it. Standing before it, feeling the sun on her shoulders and the breeze in her hair, smelling the dry earthy, stony smell of it, Dusa drank it in. Behind her, Yali nodded to Teno, who nodded back.

Dusa spoke at last. "Now I know why you want all day to be here," she said.

"Yes," Yali agreed, continuing after a moment, "I think this is the best view, at present. Long ago, all views were marvelous. Nowadays, the scientists are busy trying to save it. From other perspectives, you can't avoid the scaffolding."

"It is nearly three thousand years old," said Teno dreamily. "Almost anything is likely to need reconstruction and restoration after all that time."

"True enough," Yali sighed. "True enough. I'm glad you feel it so deeply, Dusa. It brings us closer. Shall we go on?"

They went on more slowly. In that timeless place, Dusa's phone call lost all urgency. They walked around three sides of the Parthenon, jostled by other sightseers, held back by ropes from walking up to touch the ancient stones.

Teno led the way to a low wall, pointing down at a vast amphitheater, far below. "The theater of Dionysos," she said, "the oldest theater in the world. We'll bring you here to see the ancient tragedies. We have our favorites. The old dramatists didn't always get the story right." She shook her head reprovingly.

Dusa could see vast rows of stone, curving down to a huge platform. From this height, it was impossible to guess how deep the seats might be, or how much space between the rows. What would make an ancient story right? or, by extension, wrong? she wondered, then dismissed the thought.

By the time they entered the museum, two and a half hours had vanished. Tour guides talked loudly in at least two different languages, and footsteps clattered on the marble floor. Dusa made a half-hearted attempt to telephone, and turned down Yali's offer to help her try again. "Let's not waste our time," she said. "I don't think it will work, and I couldn't hear anything if it did."

They looked at some of the marble friezes, protected here from wind and acid rain and the touch of millions of curious hands, but the great carvings lost much of their power in the crowded, noisy place. When Yali asked if Dusa was ready to go, she said yes thankfully.

They located their taxi easily, careened through narrow streets, and found themselves once more bowling along a boulevard at a pace exhilarating and terrifying by turns. On their right, the ocean crashed. Occasionally, Dusa glimpsed a beach. She had washed as best she could on the plane, but the waves reminded her how badly she wanted a shower, or a swim.

"Do you swim every day at the island?" she asked.

"Before breakfast, when the weather is warm," replied Teno. "Come down with me tomorrow, if you like."

"Do the other girls swim too?" asked Dusa. Teno and Yali had not said a word about the others. "How many others are there? Do we share the showers?" Dusa laughed, wondering why she felt so awkward, asking.

"The tower room has its own Jacuzzi and separate shower," said Teno. "That's the room we think you'd like." She paused. "Dusa, remember what we've told you about our project. That's why you're here. Don't think about other people. They aren't important."

Dusa was quiet, but now her mind worked more busily than ever. Not think about the others? What on earth did Teno mean? The Jacuzzi sounded wonderful, though, and the shower.

The Cessna was moored at a dock, like a powerboat or a yacht, rocking gently on its pontoons. Compared to the Boeing, this plane was minuscule! At sight of it, the notion of a quick dip vanished from Dusa's mind. The little aircraft sparkled in white, with a jaunty red stripe along the side. What fun it would be to tell Mom about this! Mom!

"Come on," said Teno. "Telephone this way."

Dusa followed the navy-suited figure into a corrugated metal shed.

"This is where you talk to your mom, while I check the plane and file my flight plan," Teno said.

"I'll come too," said Yali. "I can talk to the operator." Dusa looked at her watch, which she had changed in Athens. What time would it be at home?

Inside the shed, Teno headed for a door with the familiar stylized skirted symbol. Dusa followed Yali to the counter. She was suddenly quite desperate to hear Pearl's much-loved voice. Behind the counter a young man in a navy jacket with a shirt and tie that could have been the twin of Teno's leaned toward her, talking in a rapid and incomprehensible staccato. Yali coughed, then broke in herself, hands fluttering.

"The phone," said the man to Dusa, "it will not cost us, that is right?"

"That's right," said Dusa. She dug in her purple day pack and found her wallet with the precious calling card.

The man looked at it doubtfully. He shrugged. "Is okay," he said. "Dr. Gordon says okay. Phone is there." He pointed.

The phone sat in a sea of papers on a desk. The man lifted a flap in the counter and beckoned Dusa to come through. Yali followed. Dusa realized suddenly that her call would have an audience.

Yali lifted the receiver of a black dial phone. Dusa vaguely remembered a rotary dial phone years ago, in her grandparents' time, not nearly as heavy-looking and out-of-date as this one. Yali talked, waited, talked some more. Toronto was in the middle of another continent, Dusa reflected, and it might as well be another world. Would this phone really carry Mom's voice such a long way? Dusa looked at her watch again. Maybe she should try the office.

At last Yali handed the receiver to Dusa. "Give the operator your card number," she said. "It's all set."

"Mom," said Dusa. "Mom." She turned her back to the others. "Sure I'm okay. No, I'm not crying," she said, wiping away the sudden tears. "It's so good to hear you, Mom. Well, I'm in Athens," and she was buoyant again, telling her mother about the planes, the food, the airport. "And Mom, I've been to the Acropolis. I've seen the Parthenon."

"I always wanted to do that," said Pearl. "When I come to visit you, maybe we'll go together."

"For sure," breathed Dusa. "Oh, Mom, I do wish you were here."

"I know," said Pearl. "Right now, you do wish I was there with you, and so do I. Oh my goodness, I do. But it's all right, darling. You won't be thinking about me all the time, and you shouldn't be. Have your adventure," she said, dear Pearl. "Have your adventure, and get rid of the snakes. I'm thankful, and I'll keep things going at home, and we'll talk, and we'll write letters," she said. "I'm glad."

Dusa did not tell her mother about the snake dream on the plane; indeed, she barely remembered it. "Mom, we're flying to the island in the little Cessna. It belongs to Yali and Teno. Teno is going to fly it."

"I heard," Pearl laughed.

"How come you never told me?" Dusa did not pause for a reply. "That's all right. It was a good surprise. Mom, I'd better go, or we'll be late getting home."

Dusa didn't notice the word she had used, but Pearl, alone in the little house in Toronto, winced. "I've got your number on the island," she said. "Teno and Yali tell me the phone is not totally reliable, but it works most of the time. Take care of yourself, darling. I love you. We'll talk soon."

"I love you too, Mom." Dusa's throat tightened on the words. She put down the receiver slowly, blinking back tears, and looked around for Teno and Yali. They were gone. The man at the counter bent over a pile of paper, pencil in hand. Dusa muttered a thank-you on her way to the door.

Outside, Teno knelt on top of the plane, pouring fuel from a big red tank into a funnel projecting above the wing. To Dusa's surprise, she had changed her navy skirt for pants, also of navy serge.

"Give me a hand with the luggage, will you, Dusa," Yali called from the open door. The plane was surprisingly steady as Dusa put her weight on the dockside pontoon, handing up their various boxes and cases. "Do you get carsick?" asked Yali. "Small planes are different from big ones. I can give you something now if you think you'll need it."

Dusa was still feeling slightly spacy. "No, thanks, I'll be fine," she said, hoping she was right. Yali helped her to board.

"Sit up front," she said, "you'll get a better view." She pointed to the seat on the right-hand side. "Buckle up," added Yali briskly, and Dusa, looking around, found a shoulder harness like a car's, not a lap belt like the ones in the big planes.

Dusa had a steering wheel in front of her like the pilot's, with the upper part of the rim missing. She reached for it, imagined herself in the air, banking first to one side, then the other. Above her, a radio squawked and a staticky voice spoke, Greek, no doubt. Dusa was starting to get used to the sound of it, though she couldn't understand a word. She didn't want to interrupt the radio message, or she'd ask Yali to teach her a little: "Please," and "Thank you" and "Where's the washroom?" would be a start.

The message finished just as Teno swung herself down with the empty gas can. She picked up her clipboard from the dock and climbed aboard. "Safety drill," she told Dusa, handing over a laminated card.

"Have you ever gone down?" asked Dusa, wondering if she would truly need to know how to protect her head and put on a lifejacket in case of a sudden descent.

"Ditched, you mean?"

Dusa nodded.

"No," said Teno. "Just regulation, Dusa, don't worry, okay." She went through her prestart checklist. Dusa was surprised how long it took. Finally, Teno pulled out a knob and turned a switch. The engine roared. Teno went through another set of checks, then throttled back. A young man in paint-stained shorts came down to the dock and loosed the mooring lines, grinning cheerfully at Dusa. Teno, earphones adjusted, gave him a thumbs-up sign and taxied out into the bay.

Dusa felt a sudden surge of happiness, intense and unexpected. She had never even sat in a small plane before, let alone flown in one, but she couldn't help feeling that Teno flew as if she had always flown, as if the plane's wings had somehow grown out of her shoulders (and wouldn't that be a sight to see!). Square, chunky Teno seemed always a bit awkward on land. She belonged in the air, totally relaxed, totally in control.

It was too noisy to talk much, though Yali tapped Dusa's shoulder a few times and pointed to something below them, a small island, or a boat, and shouted a comment. Soon clouds moved across the sun, and wisps of cloud obscured the sea beneath them. Dusa's eyes were mesmerized by the gauges in front of Teno and herself, even though she had no notion what message most of them carried. "Fuel," that one was obvious, the needle reassuringly over to the right. If this flight went on forever, she would be content.

𝄂𝄂𝄂𝄂𝄂𝄂 CHAPTER 4

I t seemed no time at all until Teno's hands moved again, the noise of the engine changed, and they began circling down. Through wisps of cloud, Dusa caught a glimpse of a white tower. She looked at her watch and did a double take: was it possible that two whole hours had passed?

Farther, much farther below, the pier she remembered from the brochure pointed its long, slim finger into the sea. As they dipped toward earth, Dusa realized that two men were waiting there. Teno's descent was as confident as every other maneuver she had made. The sea rippled, but the plane moved quickly and smoothly from air to ocean until it rocked gently in the waves. Teno taxied toward shore, cutting power at exactly the right instant to bring the little aircraft alongside the dock.

"I wish I could do that," said Dusa fervently.

Smiling, Teno released the catch and opened the door beside her, hopping out briskly and taking a long step up to the pier. "Okay, Dusa, you're next," she said. "One foot on the brace, then step down to the pontoon."

Dusa eased down gingerly, one hand on the plane behind her, for balance. The little Cessna rocked slightly in the swell. The long pier was fixed in place, its wooden deck supported by huge pilings. It was a good foot higher than the pontoon, and the ribbon of water between her and it seemed dangerously wide.

Above her, a swarthy hook-nosed man extended a dirty hand. He grinned at her, and Dusa shrank back from the sudden revelation of his black gap-toothed mouth. Then she made an effort and summoned her own grin. The man's arm was strong and sure, and Dusa was glad of his support.

Ahead of her was the island. Dusa planted her feet firmly and looked up. All she could see was the dark cliff, obscurely threatening, and the stairway, a diminishing gray zigzag against the looming precipice. To her left, the cliff lowered in giant craggy steps to a point of land where several pine trees had found crevices and enough soil to grow. To her right, wooden steps went down from the pier to a little sandy beach. Beyond it, jagged rocks and black cliffs continued. On a sunny day, it would be magical, but Dusa found herself anxious to reach the top, with its terraces and the house.

Yali, a good five inches taller than Dusa, stepped from the pontoon to the dock with no assistance. The man who had helped Dusa let his hand fall; his eyes dropped, and his mouth tightened. He started to talk to Yali, a spate of language in which Dusa understood no single word. Teno, however, whirled around, looking shocked. She and Yali both started talking at the same time, fast and angrily.

The other man looked up from the mooring lines. In one startled glance, Dusa realized he wasn't much older than she was, slim, wearing baggy shorts and an old khaki shirt with rolled-up sleeves. The sun touched his red-brown hair with glints of gold. He was bronzed and beautiful, with the sun gleaming on his short chestnut curls—beautiful, that is, except for his surly face. His sullen brown eyes lingered on Dusa for a moment, and he pursed his disapproving lips.

Dusa blinked back tears, surprised by her sharp disappointment. Why? She didn't even know him. Why was a boy here anyway? Dusa knew that snake dreamers were always female.

Around them, three people screamed at each other. Everybody talked at once, more and more loudly, accompanied by furiously waving arms. Dusa waited, staring at nothing. What on earth was wrong?

At last Yali strode back to Dusa. "What's the matter?" quavered the girl.

Yali's mouth was pursed, as if she had clamped it shut with her teeth. She snorted angrily. "Trouble," she grunted. "We may be busy for a day or two, Teno and I."

Her eyes passed over Dusa as if the girl wasn't even there. She shouted to the two male figures, who came on the run, with Teno just behind. The boy jumped to the pontoon and up into the plane, where he quickly handed out suitcases and boxes. Sullenly, the older man piled them on the pier. Then, without a word, they loaded boxes on each others' backs, took two suitcases in each hand, and trod heavily over to the staircase that snaked its zigzag way dizzily up the cliff. Their boots clanged on its metal treads.

On the far side of the pier, three boats were moored. Dusa stared at them. She was shocked and horribly embarrassed, and frightened. Her eyes fixed on the largest of the boats, an elegant cabin cruiser. "Yeree-ail," she read the name aloud. Thank goodness it was written in script she could understand.

"Yer-EE-a-lee," corrected Teno's voice.

Dusa turned.

"Beautiful name, isn't it. But that's not what you're wondering about. Yali and I are upset, Dusa, and I for one don't want to stand around down here trying to explain."

"We need to get up to the house," Yali agreed. "Come along, Dusa. I'm sorry your introduction isn't perfect. We'll get it sorted out."

Dusa, thoughts and feelings in a jumble, followed Teno. What had the older man said? Why did the young one look away from her, like she had done something wrong? Why were Yali and Teno so upset?

Dusa could not begin to guess. *Euryale:* where had she heard that name before? English class? Something hovered for a moment on the edge of her memory; then she lost it, tramping up the stairs after Teno.

On this leg of the climb, and on every alternate leg, the gray stairs were built some four feet out from the cliff and parallel to it; the black rock was on Dusa's left. Had human hands smoothed its contours? Dusa had never seen a natural rock face that looked so much like a wall. She counted ten steps up to a little platform. Steel? Aluminum? Heavy metal!

Dusa grinned. She felt light-headed. Did the world's natural laws apply in this place? Did the other girls feel as strange as she did on these stairs? Adrenaline carried her more than halfway up, but the rush subsided, and Dusa felt her heart beat faster as she climbed. Soon she had to stop to catch her breath. Suspended in the air, she felt less tense. A light breeze ruffled her hair and raised goose bumps on her arms. From this height, the cliff was big, but no longer frightening.

"You're doing fine," Yali encouraged her. "The first time's the worst. You'll be running up and down in a few days."

"Sure, sure," gasped Dusa. She promised herself she would work out on those stairs until it was true. It was a long time since she'd been in such rotten condition. They weren't even close to the top when they met the two men coming down. Teno moved against the outer railing to let them pass. The men seemed to paste themselves against the dark rock face.

Yali spoke to the younger one in a flood of Greek. He nodded, without raising his eyes. "Dusa, this is Perse," said Yali. "With the news we've had, Teno and I will be busier than we expected. We'll get Perse to show you around the island. He does speak a word or two of English, don't you, Perse."

"Yes, *despinis mou*," said the young man. "I will come." His voice was flat, devoid of emotion, but there was an unfriendly glint in his dark brown eyes as they met Dusa's upward gaze, and his full, red lips bore not the tiniest hint of a smile.

Quickly they squeezed by. Dusa heard their footsteps fading away below, and then the sound of a motor. One of the boats, a workaday open craft, headed out to sea.

"Who is Perse?" asked Dusa. "He's cute." Even if he's not friendly, she added silently. Dusa wished, as so often before, that she was not so horribly shy with boys. If only she had had a brother, an older brother. Grandpa had been the only man in her life, and he had been too old to teach her about boys.

Yali looked at her curiously. "Cute?" she said. "I suppose so. It won't last. In twenty years, he'll look like his father."

Dusa made a face. The older man was seamed with age, his mouth black where teeth were missing. "Where do they live?" she asked.

"At the end of the island," said Yali, pointing. "There has always been a family there, two or three people who work for us. A boy goes to another island for a wife, or a girl for a husband, and they have a child, sometimes two children, never more. They bring supplies, do the gardening and keep the place in order. We don't care for outsiders here."

She frowned, and Teno continued. "Right now, we're very angry with Dictys and Perse. You need somebody to show you around, and we'll be busy, so Yali asked him. But I wouldn't get too friendly. Perse is just an island boy, and you won't see much of him when we begin your treatment." She nodded at Dusa, and her footsteps clanged again on the metal treads.

The next leg of the zigzag hugged the cliffside. The railing on Dusa's right was bolted with heavy steel set into the solid rock. A little breeze whipped at her clothes. Quarter turn left, one step forward, quarter turn left again, three easy steps on the level, and up, like a lopsided corkscrew. Dusa's mind fell into a sort of suspended animation. She was conscious only of her legs and her lungs. Back and forth on the steps, she climbed and turned.

Just when it seemed she could go on no longer, Dusa stepped onto the next platform, turned and found herself facing a terraced garden, bright with poppies and marigolds as well as shrubs, flowers and many small trees she could not recognize. Not far above her gleamed the white towered house. House? Mansion, rather, or castle, a small stuccoed castle with battlements, and a tower at each end. Her heart expanded instantly and encompassed the place.

Teño had turned toward her, smiling.

"It's magnificent," said Dusa. "Unbelievable." She searched for words, then gave up and stared, exalted and entranced. The clouds had rolled away again. The altercation on the landing was forgotten. A fairy-tale castle sparkled in the sunlight against the deep blue October sky. Before long the sun would set. Dusa could see already the hint of a rosy sunset glow reflected on the gleaming walls.

"Come along, then," said Yali, laughing. "Welcome to the Gordon Clinic. We're putting you in the south tower, Dusa, over the breakfast room."

"You'll love it," Teno asserted, and Dusa, still lost in

delight, felt only a slight, momentary irritation at being told in advance how she was expected to feel.

Suitcases and boxes were set neatly on the stoop at the front door. The door, rounded at the top, was constructed of heavy wooden slabs, held together by two bands of iron. Dusa thought it should be unlocked with a huge iron key, but Yali used a modern silver-colored one. Inside, she pushed buttons on a small panel. "Security system," she explained. Her mouth tightened. She looked angrily at it. "It should not have been on." She turned away, high heels clicking on green-veined marble tiles as she trotted over to a heavy antique mahogany desk.

The desktop was cluttered with telephone and answering machine, notepads, triple-tiered in- and out-baskets and other office paraphernalia. The monitor for a computer winked at Dusa from a stand placed at right angles to the desk. In an odd way the foyer reminded Dusa of the admitting area at the hospital, although the clinic was beautiful and it did not smell of disinfectant.

Yali picked up a small notebook and glanced at it. She made a face at Teno. "It's just what Dictys told us," she said grimly.

Teno frowned. "Yali, why don't you take Dusa to the breakfast room," she said. "I'll join you soon."

Yali nodded. She picked up Dusa's heavy suitcase as if it was a feather. Carrying it, she marched across the foyer and turned to the right along a wood-paneled corridor.

Dusa picked up her smaller bag and slung her day pack over her shoulder. She followed Yali. "On the left, kitchen and main dining room," Yali announced as they passed.

"On the right, exercise room and physiotherapy. Lavatory." The doors had frosted glass panels, so Dusa could not see into the rooms, and Yali did not open them. Would the mystery be explained soon? Dusa felt tense again.

The corridor led into a big, high-ceilinged circular room. When she stepped through the door, Dusa was dazzled by the glory of the late-afternoon sun, already making a path of gold across the sea far below. She turned slightly, so as not to be gazing directly into the light. In front of her and around almost the entire room, there were no solid walls, but only windows, soaring narrow uncurtained panes of glass. At the bottom of each segment, a low unscreened casement could be opened.

"Oh, Yali!" The mood of exaltation caught Dusa again and left her once more without words.

"This is the breakfast room," said Yali.

The soft voice seemed to Dusa a signal to look away from the windows, and she gave her attention to the room. Near the corridor, an iron staircase twisted upward, disappearing into an oblong hole in the ceiling. Was this the way to her room? she wondered. Bright chintz-covered wing chairs and a love seat made a sort of horseshoe facing the ocean. Padded seats encircled the room under the windows. In the middle of the room were three pretty glass-topped white wicker dining tables, each with four matching chairs.

Dusa looked, and looked again. There was no mess, no clutter of girls' stuff, tapes, cassettes, hairbands, earrings or magazines, nothing personal at all. No one had rushed to meet them at the door. The door had been locked, and the security system had been turned on. Except for their own footsteps and their own voices, Dusa had heard no human sound. In the gracious, elegantly furnished room, Dusa felt slightly sick, and very much alone. She faced Yali. "Where is everybody?" she asked. "What's wrong?"

They both heard Teno's footsteps, and she erupted into the room as Dusa spoke. "They've gone," Teno growled. "That's what's wrong. What a thing to come home to!"

"It's not the welcome we planned, Dusa." Yali sighed.

"Who's gone?"

"Our entire staff," said Yali. "That's right, isn't it, Teno? Three patients, too."

Teno nodded.

Yali went on. "That was what Dictys told us. I still can't take it in. We talked to Diana—when was it, Teno? Three days ago?"

"Did you phone, Yali, or did she?"

Yali pondered. "She did, the scheming witch! She told me the phone had been acting up, not to worry if we couldn't get through. Likely she wasn't calling from here at all!"

"She'll be sorry." All around Teno was a glittering aura of danger. "Oh yes, Yali, she'll be sorry she was ever born."

Dusa shivered. "How could they?" she faltered.

Teno's angry face was turned toward her. " 'How' is easy enough," she snorted. "They got that fool Dictys and his idiot son Perse to take them out to the nearest place they could catch a ship. 'Diana told us it was your orders,' " she mimicked Dictys savagely. " 'She had your seal, what else could we do?' "

"He must have suspected something," said Yali

thoughtfully. "He knows us better than that. Any other time, it would have been impossible—too many patients, and most of them too sick."

"That Diana," Teno went on, as if Yali had not spoken. "We should have fired her a year ago."

"She'd have sued," Yali retorted. "Then we wouldn't have made our speech in Toronto and we wouldn't have met Dusa. We thought she had changed, Dusa. We are not usually fooled."

No, thought Dusa, as Yali's eyes burned into her face, I bet you're hardly ever fooled. For sure, I wouldn't want to try!

"Diana must have been thinking about this all the time," said Teno bitterly. "She was a good manager, a good psychologist, I'll give her that, she just didn't understand."

"She understood," said Yali. "When we stopped taking new patients, she didn't agree. Teno, let's not discuss it anymore. Poor Dusa, you must be wondering what kind of place you've come to!"

Dusa felt her face turning red. She felt thoroughly confused. Why wouldn't Yali and Teno want to help as many snake dreamers as they could? "I think it's awful, everybody leaving like that." Dusa was emphatic. She was also scared. What would happen to her?

"It is dreadful," Teno agreed. "It would be dreadful for the patients too, if they were not so close to full recovery." She was calm now; the glimmer of danger had disappeared. "It's not the thing to say, these days," she added, "but it's the kind of behavior I might expect from a man." She pondered, then grinned. "You don't think Diana should have been called Giorgios, or Spyridon, do you? I never examined her."

Dusa goggled. "You can't be serious."

Teno giggled, an oddly horrifying sound from her square crimson mouth. "No," she said, "she didn't need to be a man, women can be traitors too."

Yali clapped her hands, and Teno started, as if rousing from a reverie. "No use wasting more energy," she said. "I am ready for dinner, bath and bed, not necessarily in that order."

Dusa nodded, very much aware that the day had been exhausting even before they reached the island. "You flew us here," she recalled, "on top of our trip to the Acropolis. Are you very tired?"

Teno shrugged. "Our housekeeper used to say, 'I'm all in but my bootlaces, and they're dragging.' I'm not quite that tired, but not far off," she admitted. "Come upstairs, Dusa." She started toward the staircase. "You can see the rest of the place later. No rush, you'll be here for a while." She spiraled up as she spoke. Dusa's big suitcase dangled on the outside of the railing, describing dizzying circles, clasped easily in Teno's stubby hand.

Dusa followed uncertainly, but her small bag bumped the railing and she tripped. Yali caught her. "Circular staircases are fine when you get used to them," she said. "Here, Dusa, give me that case."

"Thanks." Dusa rubbed her arm. "What strong hands you have, Grandma."

Yali raised her eyebrows and Dusa blushed. They both laughed, and Dusa's stomach righted itself. She was here to help with a research project, and to be cured. Whatever needed to be sorted out, no doubt it would be sorted out. All in good time.

With only her day pack, Dusa climbed upstairs easily. "Oh!" She caught her breath. Windows encircled the spacious room, and the view was even more amazing than from the room below! She walked forward, her rubber-soled feet silent on unglazed terracotta tile, and knelt on the window seat, looking down where the lowering sun threw a long golden beam across the azure sea.

Dusa exhaled slowly, her inner turmoil beginning to subside. After a silent minute she turned away from the windows to survey the room. A big, low bed faced her, its bookcase headboard flat against an inner wall, rush mats on either side. A large tape deck/CD player projected over the edge of one night table, with an immense chest of drawers and wardrobe beyond. The other night table was bare, except for a starkly modern reading light. A dark wooden writing table with carved legs and matching chair adjoined it.

"I love this room," Dusa said.

"We hoped you would." Teno sounded relieved and pleased.

"Is there anything else you'd really like?" asked Yali. "I wondered about an easy chair."

Dusa looked at the cushions piled here and there on the padded window seat and shook her head. "There's only one thing," she said wistfully. "It's about three times as big as my room at home." Yali's face fell. "It's a great room, don't get me wrong," said Dusa quickly. "I just don't want to get lost."

Yali nodded. "I think you'll get used to it quickly," she

said. "If it doesn't feel good after a few days, there are smaller rooms in the main building. But this one is special."

"It sure is," said Dusa fervently. "I think it's going to be fine, Yali."

"If it's not, we'll change things until we get it right," said Yali again.

Dusa nodded thankfully. Downstairs, Teno had been scary. Yali too, though not so much. Now they were behaving the way she would expect, in spite of their own problems. "Where do you sleep?" she asked, thinking suddenly of her room at home with Pearl next door, rushing in night after night to hold her and drive away the snakes.

"We have the same room as this one," said Teno, "in the other tower, above our office."

"It's okay, Dusa," put in Yali softly, as if she had again been listening to Dusa's thoughts. "Don't be afraid. You won't have nightmares here, or if you do—unlikely, I assure you—Teno or I will come at once.

"One of us will monitor you—not every minute, we don't have the staff—but regularly. If you scream or start to toss about in your sleep, we'll hear you, even if we are not watching at that moment. If you're afraid an attack might be coming on, if you want our attention for any reason at all, send us a signal." She went quickly to the bed. "Look, here on your headboard. Press this button, and the alarm will ring in our room, and also on our beepers. We'll hear you, wherever we are. If we're in our room or in the office, we'll see you as well."

The slim finger pointed again, and Dusa looked up to see a small concave mirror in the angle between wall and ceiling, the kind of mirror that a store might use to catch a thief.

"That mirror is connected to a TV monitor in our rooms," Yali continued. "We can see if you're in trouble. Trust us, Dusa, and don't worry. You are safe here with us."

Teno spoke very softly. Dusa thought she said, "In this place, the snakes will be your friends. You will learn to welcome them." At that moment, Dusa felt only a huge surge of relief.

"Here's your bathroom," Yali announced, throwing open a door that had been partly hidden by the wardrobe.

"Oh my goodness," Dusa gasped. This room was no larger than the bathroom at home, but luxurious far beyond anything Dusa had seen. The Jacuzzi tub, like the oval washbasin on its pedestal, was made of pink-veined marble, and a marble shelf held an assortment of shampoos, bath oils and other toiletries. Even the toilet matched! A corner shower stall was made of glass, walls and door forming half a hexagon. All the taps were gold, and very elaborate. Bright light reflected on mirrored walls. There were no windows, but Dusa had no feeling of claustrophobia. Bemused, she opened the shower door. "Amazing," she said, forgetting that she had given up the word. "I'd be scared to use it." She laughed self-consciously. "I'd mess it up."

"Enjoy," said Teno. "That's what it's for."

Dusa put down the thick pink bath towel and went back into the bedroom, ready to open her suitcase and pull out her nightshirt. The circular staircase continued its upward spiral to another hole in the ceiling. "What's up there?" Dusa asked. "Another room?"

Yali nodded. "We thought you'd prefer this one," she said. "It's brighter, and the bathroom is prettier, but"—she shrugged—"let's take a very quick look."

This tower room seemed much smaller than the room below. Straight walls rose only shoulder high before sloping steeply inward to meet in a point, like the inside of a giant ice-cream cone. Here too were windows and a window seat, but here the seat was only a few inches above the floor, and the windows were low and dark.

This room was full of mystery; the high vault seemed to cast shadows everywhere. The room was pleasantly furnished. In another mood, Dusa might have loved its enclosed space. Now she shook her head, wondering why she felt uneasy here, wishing there was a trapdoor so that she could shut this room off from the one she would be living in, just below. Climbing quickly down, she felt the shadows pursuing her, although they were soon dispelled by the bright room beneath. Behind her, Yali and Teno exchanged a satisfied glance.

"I'll bring your dinner here on a tray tonight," said Yali. "We all need to get to bed. Do you mind?"

"Of course not," said Dusa. "I'll unpack some of my stuff while I wait."

██████████ CHAPTER 5

D usa was almost too tired to eat, though Yali brought
the tray fairly quickly, and an enticing odor rose
from the covered dish. Dusa lifted the lid and
sniffed, then breathed more deeply.

"*Tavas,*" said Yali, smiling. "Lamb stew. Okay?"

Dusa nodded. If it tasted as good as it smelled, more
than okay.

"Put the lid back on for a minute," said Yali. "I'll show
you how to run the shower and the Jacuzzi. Is your tooth-
brush unpacked? Is everything all right?"

Dusa's bare feet felt cold on the tile floor. Impulsively,
the girl held out her arms, and Yali, with a smile at once
wry and tender, stepped close. Dusa felt herself clasped by
arms of steel, held against a body that seemed to consist of
nothing but muscle and bone. How different from her
mother's plump arms and the yielding softness of her
mother's breast! "You're strong." Dusa's impromptu admi-
ration was muffled by Yali's shoulder.

"I'm very strong," Yali murmured, her soft breath warm

on Dusa's curls. The tall woman patted the girl's thin shoulder and turned away with a quick, "Sleep well, Dusa, see you in the morning."

Dusa took one mouthful of the stew, and another. *Tavas*, did she remember it right? The fork kept moving automatically to her mouth until suddenly only the gravy remained. She picked up the spoon and finished that as well. Then she took a quick shower, dried off some of the remaining grime on the pink towel, made a face at it and tumbled into bed. Tonight she would be asleep before her head hit the pillow, in two shakes of a lamb's tail. Her mother used the first expression; her grandfather had used the second. Mom. Grandpa.

Dusa did not fall asleep. Thoughts crowded in and would not be pushed away. The view of the island, as she had seen it from the air when they started their descent, came back to her mind. She thought she'd seen the whole place, though apparently she'd missed the house where Dictys and Perse lived; it couldn't be very big.

Dusa had seen trees and rock, plenty of both, but no sign of habitation except this building and its pier; no other building, no other docks or boats, and except for the tiny strip of dark sand beside the landing, not even a beach. For whatever reason, the staff had deserted. There were no other patients. Aside from two scared-looking men who had promptly departed, she had seen no sign of human life, except of course for the two sisters who had brought her. Whatever would happen next, she was alone with them. She was alone.

Sudden panic struck. Dusa's face turned clammy. Under the feather duvet, she shivered uncontrollably. She curled into a ball, pulled the bedclothes over her head, and did not push the button on the headboard. She'd learn to welcome the snakes, would she? Never! What treatment had she let herself in for? What did she and Pearl know about the Gordons? Could she really trust them? Was she in a clinic or a jail? Would the telephone work?

The glory of the Parthenon was totally forgotten. Dusa had had enough of this adventure, enough of Teno and Yali. What if they really wanted, for some reason of their own, to encourage the snakes, not to get rid of them at all? She felt the creatures stirring at her thought, and managed, with enormous effort, to stop thinking about them. This was her only possible defensive strategy, and most of the time it didn't work. Dusa thought about her mother, visualized Pearl's arms around her and held the vision, but the panic stayed with her, just under the surface, even after she finally fell into a restless sleep.

In the morning, Dusa's empty stomach woke her. Her little clock said 8:00 A.M. Last night's panic had left her. She no longer felt anxious, only hungry. Yawning, she dashed cold water on her face. She put on her blue terry robe over her striped nightshirt and went down. The day was again bright; already the sun was warm. A round, white-enameled openwork iron table on the terrace outside the breakfast room was set for breakfast for three. Teno, seated, scooped out grapefruit with a pointed spoon. Yali bustled out with a loaded tray.

"What are you going to do about the others?" Dusa asked.

"The deserters?" queried Yali. "We'll begin by phoning our lawyer in Athens and getting his advice, then we will start work with you. That's our plan for this morning. Soon, Teno and I must find out where the girls are and how they are doing. We are responsible for them. Then we must call their guardians. I'm not looking forward to any of this, Dusa, but it's not going to muck up our project. We won't allow it."

"No indeed," Teno agreed. "It may even be for the best; now there's nobody to get in our way. One phone call, Dusa, and then you will have our total attention."

Suddenly Dusa did not feel hungry after all. Yesterday, she had planned to swim with Teno before breakfast. She managed half a grapefruit and a spoonful of scrambled eggs, nothing more. Teno and Yali did not press her.

"I'll phone Athens if you like," said Teno to her sister.

"Good," Yali agreed. "Dusa, I'll get us settled in the office."

The office corridor led off the foyer, opposite the corridor to the breakfast room. "We wanted to begin right away," Yali said. "The sooner we get your illness under control, the better."

"That's why I'm here," Dusa agreed, disconcerted by her sudden reluctance. Of course that was why she was here. Why did she have to force her feet to follow Yali's tapping high-heeled shoes?

The office occupied the ground floor of the north tower. The room was the twin of the breakfast room, except that its aspect was reversed, but it seemed even larger. Here the bay windows looking out to the ocean were not lined with seats. Three big reclining chairs of butter-soft beige leather occupied the central part of the room.

To Dusa's right, toward one of the flat walls, stood a

huge black pedestal desk topped with a slab of thick black glass. A starkly modern pen stand and three-tier organizer tray gleamed in silver color, reflected faintly in the dark, uncluttered surface of the desktop. The modern note was completed by a black computer stand with hutch, loaded with equipment. Dusa's eyes widened as she took in the size of the monitor.

Two black horizontal file cabinets hugged the wall behind the desk. To the left of them, a door stood ajar.

"What's that?" Dusa pointed.

"Office storage, dead files, old stuff."

"That's not what I meant." Dusa walked slowly toward the door. Yali followed. The door had been forced open. It was a heavy door, and it looked undamaged, but there was a jagged break in the frame. They stared at it. Yali swore. She strode past Dusa into the storage room.

Dusa bent to examine the damage.

"I can fix this," she said to Yali's back. "Where do you keep your tools?"

Yali laughed shortly.

"I can," repeated Dusa. "I need a piece of two-by-four, it doesn't have to be very long, and some of this framing. Hammer and nails and a little paint and it'll be as good as new."

"You can do this yourself?" Yali turned, amusement replacing the rage in her eyes.

"Sure," Dusa replied. "Grandpa always let me help him. After he died, I went on doing things. Mom says I've saved her a ton of money."

"Thanks for the offer," said Yali. "I'm tempted to let you do it, Dusa, but it's really Dictys's job. He's got the tools, and he knows where to find the lumber. The damage made me angry, and the invasion here. I can't see anything out of place, but who knows? Teno and I will have to go through all the files, everything in the room. What were they trying to do?" She turned back to the office, beckoning Dusa to follow, and gestured to a chair.

"Sit down, Dusa," she said. "That forced entry is just another nuisance to forget about for now. We came here to start helping you." She paused.

"To begin, let me tell you about our treatment. Of course, each person is unique. As we get to know you better, we will adjust the program to your needs. We talked this through with your mother, Dusa, so she knows about it."

"What about your research project?" asked Dusa. "Does that change anything?"

"Good question. It will not change the course of treatment so much as our monitoring and recording of it. Every session will be recorded, on videotape and on audiotape. We will ask you to record your activities, your feelings, and of course your dreams. Those dreams, Dusa, I expect them to be extremely illuminating."

Dusa shivered.

"That prospect frightens you, doesn't it."

Dusa nodded. Her throat was dry. She tried to swallow, and failed.

"You have come here to get better," said Yali.

Dusa nodded again.

"Concentrate on that," said Yali kindly. "Everything we do here will help you to get better. Keep that in your mind. Shall I go on?"

Dusa gulped. "Yes, please, Yali."

Yali nodded thoughtfully. "There are three main strands in our treatment. I could describe them as psychological, medical and physiological. Much of our work together is psychological, exploring your relationship with your snakes, if I may put it thus. We must understand you very well indeed, Dusa, you and your ancestry, your feelings. In the beginning, the snakes themselves will lead us. We will talk with you. We will hypnotize you. We will regress you, leading you back through this life, through your birth, back, and back and back."

Yali's soft voice was thrilling. Dusa felt herself vibrating with it, as if her whole self was a drum.

Footsteps jarred, breaking the mood. Dusa blinked.

Teno, notebook and pen in hand, gave Yali an "okay" thumb and first finger joined in a circle, and sank into the third chair.

"I was giving Dusa an overview," said Yali, in her usual pleasant tone. "We found some damage here, they forced the door of the storage room, but you and I can deal with it later. Why don't you tell Dusa a little about our medical treatment?"

"Much damage?"

"Not obviously."

"Okay." Teno turned to Dusa. "Do you remember the pill I gave you on the plane?"

Dusa frowned.

"Like this." Teno shook out another purple capsule.

Dusa nodded, though she didn't remember anything very clearly.

"We have several medications to control the snakes, or

to encourage them, depending on the situation. The pills are most useful in early stages of treatment, especially with patients whose illness is more advanced than yours before they come to us. Do you feel more comfortable, Dusa, knowing that you do not have to fight the snakes off all by yourself?"

"Oh yes," Dusa breathed.

"Security," Teno smiled, "the pills give security, that's the most useful thing about them. Did Yali tell you about the physiological strand?"

Dusa shook her head.

"You must build up stamina," said Teno. "We focus on exercise and diet. I'm sorry for your sake we've lost our physiotherapist, she was very good. We'll manage, though. With you, Dusa, we may make more use of the ocean than the gym. You like the water, don't you."

"Love it." Dusa relaxed. "Mom says, come summer, I'm in the water more than I'm out. When I'm not climbing, that is."

"Ah," Yali purred, "you like to swim, and you like to climb. You came to the right place, didn't you." She chuckled. "I can see us building up your stamina through some of the things Teno and I do for relaxation, Dusa. Archaeology is our hobby, underwater archaeology especially."

"It was in the brochure." Is there anything these two can't do? Dusa wondered idly.

"Any questions?" asked Yali.

Dusa smiled. Once more, Yali seemed to be reading her mind. "Not right now," she said.

"Tilt your chair back, then. Let's be comfortable."

The rest of the morning passed in a blur. Dusa talked and talked: friends, school, things she loved, things she hated, anger, fear. Skillful questions led her back through childhood years, in the time before snakes. Grandpa and Grandma came to life again. She felt Grandpa's arms around her, his tweed vest rough against her face, and cried uncontrollably. She heard Grandma's voice, telling how she came to Toronto, and cried again. By noon, she was wrung out.

"We've worked hard," said Yali. "Well done, Dusa. That's enough for today."

Dusa lay in the chair for a minute or two before summoning the energy to sit upright. She looked at Teno and Yali. Strange creatures, even though they seemed to care about her. Even here, in their own home, Teno wore the navy trouser suit, white shirt and tie. Except that the suit seemed always pressed, the shirt always fresh, and the skirt had turned into pants, Teno might have worn the same clothes every day since Dusa had met her. Did she never tire of them? At least today Teno wasn't acting weird.

So far Yali had not worn the same ensemble a second time. Her outfits were always exotic; again today, in an ankle-length white and gold tunic with matching slingbacks, she could have stepped out of a fashion magazine. Where did the money come from?

"You must be millionaires," Dusa blurted out her thought.

"We are wealthy," Teno agreed, showing no surprise. "We can afford to fund this research, if that's what you have been wondering. We lived here long before there were written records. This property has always been ours."

"A very old family," agreed Yali. "Are you ready to get up now, Dusa? It's time for lunch. Then you can go exploring while Teno and I make our phone calls." She made a face at the prospect.

"The island isn't huge. You'll learn your way around very quickly. Look on the terrace, do you see the bell? I'll ring it for you at five-thirty. Dinner will be ready at six." She pointed. Dusa could see the iron bell, a foot tall or more, suspended from a wooden frame.

"Did you buy hiking boots?" asked Teno.

Dusa nodded.

"Wear them," said Teno. "Be very careful, Dusa, we can't have you getting hurt. I think we should give her a beeper, Yali, in case she falls sometime."

Dusa was vaguely surprised. Teno had not struck her as a mother-hen type. "Our house in Toronto isn't far from the bluffs," she said. "I've been climbing since I could walk. Don't worry about me."

"I'm sure you're fine," said Yali, "but Teno has a point. I'd feel better if you're not alone, at least until you get to know the place. Perse can go with you this afternoon. I'll let him know."

"Perse!" Teno snorted derisively. "Don't be a fool, Yali. Perse thinks too much of himself already."

"I don't think he likes me," said Dusa hesitantly.

Teno looked at her in exasperation. "Likes you! He's a servant, Dusa, his ancestors were our slaves."

Yali laughed. "Sister dear," she said, "how can you expect a modern young woman to see these things the way you do? You won't be seeing much of Perse, Dusa—you have other things to do, and so does he—but you've been in hospital, you haven't done much climbing recently, so let's play safe today." In one sinuous motion she stood up and started to walk; Dusa heard her sandals tap-tapping down the corridor.

"Don't be surprised if you see a snake," said Teno suddenly, "a real one."

Dusa jumped; her skin prickled.

"Foolish child!" Teno's voice was impatient. "You may not see one at all, and if you do, it won't hurt you. The snakes on our island are not poisonous, and they're better than cats for killing the mice. We're glad to have them here."

🪟🪟🪟🪟🪟🪟🪟 CHAPTER 6

Dusa went climbing by herself after all. Perse and his father could not be reached. Teno eventually took the small boat and went in search of them, returning with the news that their hut was empty and their boat was gone.

"I expect they're fishing," said Yali. "I'll have a talk with Dictys, they have no business going off without letting us know. Be extra careful, Dusa."

Dusa nodded, relieved that the sullen young man would not be with her.

The island seemed to consist of one high plateau surrounded by steep cliffs. The cliffs were punctuated by slopes, some larger, some smaller, falling sharply to the waves. Flowers grew in every cranny of the rocks, and Dusa decided to pick a bouquet of poppies later, on her way back.

After several false starts, she found a place to begin her climb. The way was steep; one could hardly call it a path. Dusa was glad of her tough jeans and heavy boots. The

October day was windless and the rock was warm enough for shorts, but shorts would not have protected her legs from rocks and brambles. Partway down, she could see a grove of trees—oaks, she thought—though they were some distance away. Idly, she began to work her way toward them.

Almost at once, she regretted her decision. This was not much like the bluffs she was used to, where the really dangerous parts were fenced and posted. Where Dusa was accustomed to climb, there was always something to hang on to—if not a tree, then a guardrail—and paths crisscrossed the slopes. Here, she was working her way across little ledges, most of them not wide enough for her to set one foot beside the other. Although she had a good head for heights, she constantly reminded herself that it was safer not to look down.

Looking sideways was bad enough, but Dusa was sure she could see places for hands and feet if she moved toward the trees. She could not see footholds all the way back, even though they must exist; after all, she had come that way. Just because they existed, however, was no reason she had to be able to find them. No, onward was better than trying to go back. Step by slow step, she moved toward the trees.

What if she could not find a way up—or down—from the grove? Dusa decided to worry about that later, if she had to. Pearl had taught her if she ever got stuck on a ledge at the bluffs, she should stay put and wait for help. She didn't want to make a fool of herself with Yali and Teno, just the same, or to make it seem that she could not be trusted to go off by herself.

At last Dusa was able to put two feet on a mossy ledge wide enough for walking. A moment more, and she stood among the trees. They were indeed oaks, but contorted and tangled, one with another. They reminded Dusa of cedars that had lodged in crevices of the granite ridges that formed the Bruce Peninsula, not far northwest of Toronto. Rooted in shallow pockets of soil, the cedars had never grown more than a few feet tall. Scientists had been amazed to discover that they were more than seven hundred years old. The oaks surrounding Dusa were much bigger than the hunched cedars, but just as violently misshapen. It was easy to believe they had been growing here on this rocky slope for more than a thousand years.

Earlier, Dusa had listened to the birds, wishing she knew their calls. Now she heard nothing except the sounds of dead leaves rustling under her feet, or a dry twig snapping. It was not truly dark under the canopy, but it was very dark compared to the brilliant sunlight on the rock face. Dusa shivered in her sweat-damp clothes.

Suddenly the explorer found herself facing an enormous oblong rock. It stood upright like a coffin on its end, or a giant tombstone, higher than she was tall. The rock was green-gray, covered with little mosses and lichens. A large oak had tilted it slightly and might in a few more centuries tip it over, Dusa thought.

Why did the place feel to her like a grave? No human hands could have brought such a headstone here! Still, her fingers wandered into crevices in the rock, and she found herself imagining an inscription. Sacred to the memory of . . . She laughed aloud. Ridiculous. Out of the blue, a thought popped into Dusa's head: Here if anywhere she would find snakes. She turned slowly in a complete circle, peering at the ground, ears alert to hear the slightest rustle. Nothing. She breathed more easily, thankful that no serpents came to trouble her here in this dark wood.

How could she get back? She stared upward through the trees. If she could get to the plateau, it would not be difficult to find her way to the house.

There was no path. It was as if no one had walked here for a thousand years. The trees themselves had long since crowded out all competing growth, however, and the ground between the vast trunks was slippery with dry leaves or spongy with moss but relatively easy walking. As the terrain grew steeper, the walking became more difficult. By the time Dusa emerged onto rock again, she was scuffing down through layers and layers of leafy muck to find her footholds. Once, then again, she sat down to catch her breath.

The rock proved easier. There was a sort of chimney, a crack in the cliff face. It was almost as easy as climbing a ladder, though Dusa suspected it would be easier to go up than to come down, unless one came down very suddenly, which would be both quick and easy, and probably terminal. She shuddered, and did not look down.

When she emerged on the plateau, another surprise awaited, this one even more astonishing than the tombstone rock. As she sat, waiting to get her breath, Dusa's eyes caught a flash of movement far below her on a narrow, craggy ledge. Was she looking at two gigantic eagles? Glittering bodies, where the sun caught them. What could they be? Almost at once, the two figures moved, on legs rather than wings, as far as she could tell, and were hidden by the bulging cliff.

"You see them." The male voice was heavily accented, but Dusa had no trouble understanding the words.

"Who's that? Come out of there, so I can see you." With clenched fists, Dusa started toward the voice, which seemed to emerge from a thicket of dense shrubs.

"No, I don't come out. Come you in," said the voice. "You see me yesterday. Perse, you know."

Dusa peered into the tangled growth. At last she saw him. A smile lit the bronze face. "Hello," she said, doubtfully.

Perse beckoned. Dusa hesitated for a minute, then shrugged and stepped into the opening where he held the bushes aside. At once he let go, and they were hidden. In the dimness, they looked at each other.

"Yesterday, why did you look at me like that?" What a dumb thing to say, thought Dusa, her face burning.

"Like what?" Perse shrugged. "Be careful with them two, me. You too, careful. Diana say no more girls are coming, then you come. Why you come here?"

Dusa gaped at him. "It is a clinic," she said stiffly. "They are doctors. I have snake dreams. They will help me, that's why I'm here."

Perse sighed. "No good," he said. "What is your name?"

"Dusa."

"Dusa!"

"That is my name. What's wrong with it?"

"You the one they want, I bet you." He sighed again. "They very strong, them two."

"You're trying to scare me," said Dusa angrily. "That's mean."

"No," said Perse. "Look, I better tell you one-two things. Other time, I maybe don't talk, they can see, they can hear, not safe, you understand?"

"I understand what you're saying," said Dusa, "but no, I don't get it, I don't understand."

Perse shrugged. "Hard to tell," he said simply. "Hard to say, and you not believe anyway, I guess."

"Maybe not," said Dusa, "but you can't stop now. I'm listening, Perse." She settled herself cross-legged on the dry leaves, elbows on her knees.

Perse leaned toward her, speaking very softly. "This island not like other place, not like Athens, not like other island, not like Crete, no. Diana want me to go away, Fader also, but we not go, no way."

"Why not?" Dusa demanded.

"Can't," said Perse glumly. "Make me feel bad bad bad. Fader also, the same."

It made no sense to Dusa. Perse's story, if he was really saying what she thought, got stranger. Teno had said his family were servants; once they had been slaves on this same island, and that seemed to be what Perse was saying as well. His grandfather had died last year. The old man had been a hundred years old, minus four years.

"Ninety-six! That's old!" Dusa was impressed.

"Yes, ninety-six," Perse agreed.

The old man had worked for Teno and Yali from the time he was a boy, helping his father, like Perse helped Dictys. Teno and Yali were the same then as now, though the patients came and left under sail. There were more staff then, his grandfather had said, all foreign; a Greek person might come, but never stayed.

"Teno and Yali?" asked Dusa. "Their grandmothers, you mean?"

"No, the same," but Perse nodded as if he was agreeing with her, his brown eyes dark and serious. "Here the old times are not dead," he told Dusa. Then his eyes flickered away.

Dusa could not think of a thing to say. She glanced at her watch. "I've got to go," she told him awkwardly.

"You not believe me."

"I don't know. It is pretty weird."

"Watch out then. Take care, Diana say to me, now I say to you, take care." His strong hands held the branches aside once more, and Dusa slipped out.

At dinner, Dusa said nothing about Perse and his strange story. Instead, she asked about the great golden birds. Teno, in her unchanging navy, raised her eyebrows. Yali, dressed now in a pantsuit of ecru lace, shrugged elegant shoulders. "We do have eagles here," she said, cool and amused, "but Dusa, they aren't giants. You might see one in a treetop, or circling in the sky—but *walking*? They hop if they have to, but they'd much rather fly. Your eyes must have tricked you. The light is so bright here, it's not surprising."

Dusa felt about ten years old. "I guess," she said, doubtfully. She was silent. The others were silent. Dusa, inexperienced in such silences, broke it first. "So, tell me about the oak trees. Are they"—she remembered her teacher's phrase—"old-growth forest?"

Yali and Teno both pounced. Had she gone into the

trees? That was dangerous, hadn't they told her to be careful? What did she see? What did she find?

"No snakes, thank goodness," said Dusa, surprised by a sudden burst of angry energy. "Not on the ground, and not in my head, and just as well—I wouldn't want anything to make me jump when I was on those cliffs." She changed the subject for a second time.

"I did find a big stone," she said quietly, "all on end, like a giant tombstone, I thought, even though I know it was silly to think that. I'm sure nobody is buried there."

"The old stories say a body *is* buried there," said Teno slowly, "a body without a head."

"Teno," Yali scolded, "that's no way to cure Dusa's nightmares. Don't let her scare you, Dusa. There's nothing to be scared about."

"True enough," said Teno. "But don't believe everything you hear, Dusa—or everything you see, either," she added, looking directly at the startled girl.

CHAPTER 7

"Today, we want to begin by hypnotizing you," said Yali the next morning, smiling at Dusa, who had gone at once to the butter-soft reclining chair. Dusa, eager to begin, had led the three of them to the office right after breakfast. After her climb the previous afternoon she had slept well. The snakes had hissed gently into her dreams for a short time, and hissed their way as gently out again. No body, headless or otherwise, had troubled her.

"I never knew anybody who was hypnotized," she said.

"You'll find it fascinating, I expect, as well as very useful," said Yali. "It may take a little time, of course. Sometimes, results are quick and dramatic." She beamed. "There is no better way to get in touch with the snakes."

"There is no better way to help Dusa get in touch with her snakes," amended Teno.

"That's what I meant, of course," Yali agreed. "You remembered so much yesterday, Dusa. It was magnificent. Now that those gates of memory are open, who knows what else may emerge? At the same time, we'll begin to tap genetic and ancestral memories, the sooner the better."

Dusa felt her eagerness evaporate. "If you hypnotize me this morning, what will you do?" she asked.

"We will summon the snakes," replied Yali.

"No!" Dusa burst out.

"Don't be afraid, Dusa, we can control them, and we will. It may be the snakes want you to do something. We must find out."

The first attempts at hypnosis did not succeed. "You are resisting, Dusa," said Teno quietly. "Trust me, let yourself go."

Dusa felt the hot blush in her face. Teno seemed endlessly patient. Again she took out a little shining pendulum and set it swinging gently back and forth while Dusa watched through unfocused dark blue eyes. Again, she told Dusa to let her eyelids droop, let herself drift, again she began to count backward, her voice lulling, willing Dusa to—to—welcome the snakes!

That day, and the next, and the next again, Teno reached this point and a terrified Dusa snapped back to full consciousness. Teno still behaved patiently, but Dusa felt tense and edgy, and was sure both sisters felt the same way. Afternoon scrambles about the island or swimming from the beach beside the pier failed to reduce the tension.

"For the next few days, we'll begin with memories and feelings," said Yali. "We'll do more of the work we know you do well. In a week, you may be ready for us to try hypnosis again."

On Sunday, Dusa swam for a bit and walked for a bit and tried to read, but she couldn't settle. "So what if it's only seven A.M. in Toronto?" said Yali at last, looking at the sandwich Dusa had nibbled and put down again. "You're like an ant on a griddle, girl. Go ahead, phone your mom. Here, this is what you have to dial, I wrote it out. Use the phone in the hall, there's nobody to get in your way."

"Thanks." Dusa hadn't known how badly she wanted to talk to her mother. The call was easy, and Pearl picked up on the very first ring.

"Mom!"

"Dusa! You're all right?"

"Sure, Mom. What's the panic? Did I wake you up?"

"I've been trying to get you for the last two days, and the damn phone, the damn phone . . ." Pearl's voice faltered.

"Mom, hey, Mom, everything is fine, and I miss you a lot." It was true, though Dusa hadn't known how deeply she missed her mother until the words were out of her mouth. "What were you phoning about?" she asked.

"That family in Australia." Mom still sounded strange, but maybe it was only the telephone, distorting her voice. "You remember, the Gordons gave me their phone number, but I mislaid it. Well, Dusa, I've been talking to them."

"So?" asked Dusa slowly. "Is something the matter?"

"It's nothing, I guess. Alison's mom and dad will love the Gordons forever, Alison would have died without them, they told me. But then I talked to Alison, and, Dusa, it was weird." A long pause.

Dusa held her breath, then let it out in a snort.

" 'Oh, they saved me, all right,' Alison said, 'but they're the ones that made me sick, you know.'

" 'What do you mean?' I asked. 'My girl went off to Greece with them last week. She's at the clinic now. But they're not making her sick, it's not three weeks since we met them, and Dusa's been sick now for a year or more.' I took some deep breaths," Pearl continued.

" 'Sure,' said Alison, 'I didn't mean anything, forget it.' And she hung up. Oh, Dusa, I didn't want to interfere, and now I am worrying you, darling, and you sound great, and I'm overreacting, aren't I?"

"Maybe, maybe not," said Dusa. "Mom, you're babbling."

"I am," said Pearl. "It's relief, that's all." She chuckled. "Your treatment is going well, that's what I needed to hear. I'm delighted. Silly of me, darling, I'm *not* going to turn into a clinging mom—but I tried and tried. Every time, the phone was busy or it rang and rang and rang and nobody answered, over and over again. I was starting to think you'd fallen off the edge of the world."

"Relax, Mom." Why was her mother going on and on about it? She had really got herself into a state. Dusa didn't think about her first night on the island, the night she had spent cowering under the bedclothes. She didn't think about Perse and his stories, or about the people who had run away. Pearl was in a panic, and Dusa needed to help.

"I haven't had an attack since I got here. And oh, Mom, you should see my room!" They talked for another twenty minutes, with Dusa doing most of the talking.

Pearl sounded okay, and Dusa promised to phone again the following week.

Dusa had intended to ask the Gordons if the phone had been out of order, but she never got around to it. If Pearl had not been able to get through, it was hardly surprising. In the afternoons, Dusa often noticed Teno or Yali at the telephone. Now and again, she asked if the missing staff and patients had been located. The two sisters had no news, however, or none that they shared with her.

Another week passed. In Dusa's head, the snakes went into a frenzy almost as soon as she closed her eyes. Three nights in a row she pressed her buzzer, and Teno brought a purple capsule. Every morning, Dusa woke up blurry and exhausted. On the fourth day she had an attack, the worst since she had punched her mother. Dusa never remembered the details of these seizures, but she knew very well what had happened: her muscles ached as if she'd run a marathon, and the afternoon was missing from her life. She remembered getting up from the table after lunch; now she lay on the window seat, covered with a blanket. Yali sat on the floor beside her; the low sun shone crimson on her silk jersey suit. Dusa could see the hands of Yali's diamond watch: it was half past five!

On Sunday, when she talked to her mother, Dusa cried and could not get the tears to stop. This time Pearl was calm and in control.

"Teno tells me you've hit a little snag," said Pearl. "She says you are doing very well, darling, and it's temporary, and I mustn't worry. Is that how you feel too?"

"I can't do what Teno wants, and it's all my fault," wept Dusa.

"We have to be patient, darling," Pearl insisted. "I am being patient, and you must be too."

"Yes, Mom," Dusa said, tears still running down her nose.

On Monday, after another night of snake terrors, another purple pill, Teno got out the pendulum again, and Dusa, more tired than ever in her life, felt herself falling into some well so deep she might never emerge. She could hear Teno's quiet, steady voice, but it got farther and farther away.

"Snakes, serpents, so many people see them as evil. Why is that, I ask you? What comes into your mind?"

Dreamily Dusa answered, "Picture, Sunday school. Garden of Eden, serpent, snake around apple tree—apple in its mouth, and Eve with her hand out, ready to take it. Evil, Satan, snake." Her voice trailed off. She breathed heavily.

"Yes," said Teno, very softly. "One serpent in a picture, not even a real one. Would you damn all snakes because of that?"

Dusa shook her head slightly.

"You know better, Dusa, you snake dreamers. You feel kinship with the snakes, the beautiful snakes."

"Deadly," muttered Dusa. "Cobra, boa constrictor."

"No, Dusa. Your snakes do not bite, and when they wrap you round, they do not tighten their hold."

Again Teno held the crystal pendulum, shimmering at the end of its bright chain. "Go deeper, child," she commanded, in a low-pitched, sonorous voice. "Now you are relaxed even more."

"Yes." Dusa's answering voice was thick and slow.

"Listen," Teno continued, "when you awaken, you will forget what I tell you now, but you will feel differently about your snakes.

"Serpents are sacred creatures, Dusa; from earliest times, it has been so. In ancient Egypt, priestesses wore snakes like bracelets on their arms. They let themselves be bitten, taking venom into their blood, a little at first, then more and more. With that venom in their veins, they saw visions, Dusa, such visions!—ah, how wise they were.

"In India, the serpent was a god. And in Greece, in the old, old times when all mortals worshipped the great goddess, her symbol was the snake."

Dusa spoke, out of her depths: "Medusa's hair was beautiful, but Athene changed it into snakes."

"Yes!" Teno's voice was sharp with rage.

Dusa quivered, and Yali leaned forward. "Calm, child, calm," she commanded. Dusa breathed deeply and settled back in the big leather chair.

"Such lovely hair—but the snakes are beautiful too," said Yali. "Athene, with all her power, could not make them otherwise."

"Serpents have power to heal as well as power to harm," Teno continued slowly. "Doctors know this. The great Asclepius himself possessed two vials of Medusa's blood. A drop from her artery cured the most deadly illness, but a drop from her vein brought instant death."

Dusa moved restlessly.

"Dusa." Teno's voice was gentle but penetrating. "When you wake up, you will no longer fear your snakes.

They intend you no harm. You will forget what we have told you about ancient times, but this you will not forget: Your snakes are not evil; your snakes intend you no harm. Are you ready?"

Dusa nodded.

"I will count back slowly, from three. When I get to one, you will awaken. Three—you are starting back to the surface; two—getting ready to wake; and one—Dusa, open your eyes."

All three sat quietly. At last Teno raised her eyebrows in question. Dusa nodded. Teno smiled. Yali smiled. Dusa, so happy she was almost light-headed, smiled back.

After that, the daily sessions were easier.

Life on the island fell into a routine. Breakfast was usually followed by a session where Dusa was hypnotized, sometimes by one sister, sometimes by the other. Yali and Teno taped the sessions, as well as taking notes. Dusa phoned her mother every Sunday, but their conversations were brief. Aside from "I love you," there wasn't much to say.

Although the days were cooler, Dusa and Yali usually swam in the afternoon, sunning themselves lazily afterward on the dark sand of the small beach or on the pier. Sometimes Teno joined them. These days, Dusa ran easily down the zigzag staircase and trotted briskly up again.

Occasionally Dusa put on jeans and hiking boots instead of her bathing suit. "Hiking," Teno might say, "good day for it. May I join you?"

It was not really a question. Dusa could hardly say no. They did not go toward the oak grove.

Perse and his father were often about, watering and weeding the terraced gardens in front of the house, or the vegetables at the back, or tending the grapevines in their long rows. They nodded politely to Dusa, or to their employers as they passed, but did not raise their eyes.

Dictys brought fish to the back door, small white or pink-fleshed fish that brought Dusa poignant memories of her grandfather, who had taken her a few precious times to fish for bass or trout. Dictys or Perse brought baskets of small brown eggs, or a chicken, newly killed, with its head drooping.

Once, Dusa was there when the chicken was delivered. Before she realized what was happening, Yali whacked off the bird's head and feet with a cleaver on the chopping block. Dusa's stomach heaved, and she ran out of the kitchen, wondering if she would ever eat chicken again.

"You modern girls," said Teno, "you are very ignorant. How do you think your food gets to the table? If we didn't have servants, you could learn to kill the chickens yourself, and to pluck and clean them as well." She looked at Dusa and laughed, not unkindly. "But we do have servants. Let's go swimming, Dusa, and work up an appetite."

Dusa was surprised, but she was hungry after her swim, and the bird, stewed with dumplings, was irresistible. Nonetheless, Dusa left the kitchen the next time a chicken was delivered, and she tried not to hear the three great thumps on the chopping block.

"The land feeds us now," said Teno, "and the sea. Soon,

winter will be here. Then we will depend on the freezer, and I'll fly to Athens for things we do not grow."

Dusa wanted to pick the beans or cut bunches of grapes. Maybe Perse would talk to her in the garden, if she was by herself. Teno turned down Dusa's offers, however. "We have servants to do this work," she insisted.

Dusa knew that the snakes came to life in her therapy sessions, even though she did not remember much when she returned from her hypnotic journeys. She knew she had not moved from the big reclining chair, but Dusa always felt she had been far away. As the days went on, the journey back seemed to become more difficult and dangerous, and Dusa felt sweat on her body when she awoke.

"The little snake was talking to me," she said one day. "When I was hypnotized, I knew his name. I knew what he was saying, every word, but now I've forgotten everything. You heard the whole thing. What was the little snake telling me? Has he been talking to me every day?"

Yali sighed. "No," she replied. "We have been tapping your ancestral memories, very remarkable memories, up to two days ago. Now your trances are deeper, and something different is happening, but we don't have a handle on it yet.

"We hear what you say, and most of it yesterday and today has been grunts and hisses," she explained. "If some of that is snake language, Dusa, we don't understand it any more than you do. So far, nothing is clear." She looked at Teno in silent appeal.

"We get a word here and there in ancient Greek," said Teno slowly, "Greek as it was spoken three thousand years ago. You are saying these words, though the voice sounds unlike yours."

"That's not possible," said Dusa flatly. "I don't know more than a word or two of modern Greek; I've never heard any other kind."

"You've never taken classic Greek at school, Dusa?"

"Never. They don't even teach it at my school." Dusa shivered. "Make it stop!" she cried.

"Even if we could make it stop," said Teno, "it would be a huge mistake. You have not had a seizure since we succeeded in hypnotizing you. You look a thousand times better than when you arrived."

"Tell me, Dusa," Yali interjected, "how do you feel now about your snakes?"

"They don't scare me so much," Dusa admitted. She stopped. "It's ridiculous," she said reluctantly, "but I think the little one would help me if he could."

"Oh yes," said Yali softly, "I'm sure you're right. Likely that's what he is trying to tell us. If you are willing, Dusa, let's try another session this afternoon."

When Teno wakened her from her trance late that afternoon, Dusa was almost too tired to open her eyes. Teno and Yali stared at her solemnly, as if in awe. Yali's golden eyes were moist. Teno dabbed at her own wet cheeks with a Kleenex.

"What?" muttered Dusa heavily. She remembered nothing, except that the snakes had come.

"You amazing child!" Teno exclaimed.

"Why? What have I done?"

"You have journeyed back today, not nine generations but fifteen times nine generations, more than three thousand years. You are the dreamer we have been searching for. We have found you at last."

Dusa blinked. "I don't know what you're saying," she said. How many generations? How many years? "Doesn't make sense. Too tired. Can't think, it doesn't make sense."

Dusa closed her eyes, then dragged them open again.

"We learned more than you could possibly believe," said Teno, "but it doesn't matter if you believe it, or if you even know about it. Sleep well, Dusa. The snakes will not come back today, or tonight either, I promise you. I'm declaring a holiday for you tomorrow."

Yali put her arm around Dusa and helped the exhausted youngster to bed. She brought a mug of hot, clear soup and held it while Dusa sipped. She eased the girl down in the big bed and tucked the coverlet around her shoulders. Dusa slept through dinnertime. She roused herself to use the bathroom, drank more hot soup and ate sandwiches from a tray that had appeared on the floor beside her, and went back to bed, sleeping dreamlessly throughout the night.

Next morning she woke early, clearheaded and full of energy. Yali was cooking breakfast. "Can I have three eggs?" asked Dusa. "I'm starving."

"Sure," said Yali. "Set the table out on the terrace, will you? I hope you remember, today you're on holiday."

Teno bustled into the big kitchen. "We talked to our lawyer yesterday evening," she told Dusa. "I'm flying to Athens after breakfast."

"They've been found!" Dusa guessed.

"Two of the patients, yes," said Yali, "and the physiotherapist."

"I'll get some answers," said Teno. "The parents are in Athens now, waiting. I'll talk to everybody, of course, but I hope to release the girls to their parents today or tomorrow. If everything goes well, I should be back by noon tomorrow."

"What about the third girl?" Dusa wondered.

"No news yet," said Teno grimly. "Fortunately, her guardian is not making a fuss, not yet. The girl was very much attached to Diana, and he knows it. So far, he has stayed in Johannesburg. 'She'll turn up,' he says. 'She always does.' He's right. She has not run away from us, but she has run away from every other place she's been during the past ten years, often two or three times. Enjoy your holiday, you two."

Yali and Dusa spent a lazy day, swimming and lying in the sun. Yali brought snorkeling gear for both of them and a bag of stale bread for the small bright blue and golden fish that nibbled the sodden pieces from their hands. Then Dusa got out her Walkman and played a couple of the tapes she had brought, film sound tracks mostly, her favorites. She played them again and again. If she closed her eyes, she could pretend she was home. Any minute, Mom would be coming through the door.

"We discharged a girl not long ago," said Yali. "She left some tapes when she went home—on the boat, I think. You might like them. I'll keep an eye out for the bag. That reminds me, I made a note to give you a tape recorder and blank tapes for recording your dreams. Some people find audiotape works better than a notebook. Give us every bit you can dredge up. You can't know what might be helpful; nor do we, until we have it."

Dusa turned the Walkman up louder and clamped the earphones tighter on her head.

"Okay," said Yali softly. "This is a holiday, and I was pushy. Sorry I mentioned it."

Dusa's daydream was shattered, all the same. She put on her shoes. "I'm going up," she told Yali. "Then I'm going hiking. By myself, Yali."

"I understand," said Yali quietly. "Be careful, Dusa. Don't let your foot slip because you're angry with me."

It was good advice, Dusa knew, but she already knew where she was going. Now that she was alone, she was going to look for Perse. She went out the kitchen door past the vegetable patch and turned toward the far end of the island, walking steadily through grassy, flower-filled meadows, avoiding rocky outcrops and prickly patches of yellow gorse, fighting an ongoing urge to lie down and fill her nostrils with the smell of grass and poppies.

Before she knew it, she had reached the far limit of the relatively flat high ground. Looking down, she saw a small clearing at the foot of the cliff, and a tiny hut, dwarfed by the ascending wall of rock. She crept to the edge of the precipice. Digging in her toes, she peered over. She had thought of making a rope ladder, but the hut was impossibly distant. Mountain climbing gear might have helped, pitons and rock hammers, if Dusa had possessed them and known how to use them, nothing less. The cliff was sheer as far as she could see it, and likely undercut by the ocean far below, where waves broke in white foam over dark rocks. Dusa's quest was in vain: surely there was no way down.

On her stomach, she wiggled back from the edge, frustrated and angrier than when she had walked away from Yali.

"Hsss."

Was it a snake? Dusa jumped up and turned wildly, trying to locate the sound.

"Here," said a voice, a human voice.

Perse! Dusa ran toward a tangle of bush, and once more Perse pushed branches aside for her.

"Why you here?" he asked simply.

"I was looking for you," said Dusa. "I've been thinking about what you said. Not that I believe you, exactly, but I want to ask you something." She burst out with it: "Perse, why did you and your dad take everyone away from here? Those girls were sick, and the others were supposed to look after them. How could you do that?"

Perse was obviously startled, but he gathered his thoughts quickly. "Okay, they want to go," he told her, "much they want to go, they go swim if we not take them."

"That's ridiculous," said Dusa, "nobody could swim away from here. There's nowhere to swim *to*!"

"Yes," Perse agreed, "there is nowhere. Please, please on your boat, they say. No, say my fader, I no want they Gordons mad at me. They cry, boo hoo, and he say no some more, and then that girl go to my fader boat and get in, and they all get in, and my fader and me, we can't make them get out.

"This boat go sink, say my fader. So take us quick, say

that Diana girl, before big waves come. Plenty things they know, them Gordons, but this thing they not know, not now. Later maybe." The boy shrugged.

"All I can say," said Dusa angrily, "is your father shouldn't have done it. It was irresponsible." Perse raised his eyebrows, and Dusa picked a shorter word. "Bad," she said flatly. "The doctors have to find those people, and it takes much time."

"So what, it takes much time," said Perse. "They got much time, them two."

"Maybe I want them to help me and they don't have time," snapped Dusa, even though it wasn't true.

"They not want to help you," retorted Perse. "They only want to help they sister."

"They can't help her," said Dusa, shocked, "she's dead. This is a stupid conversation." She burst out of the bushes, not waiting for Perse to hold them open, and almost ran back to the house, paying not the least attention to the sights or the odors, though the grass and the flowers were no less enticing than before. Boys! Dusa was no more comfortable with Perse than with the guys back home. Arrogant, self-righteous know-it-alls, him and his dad— taking everybody away from the island, and they weren't even sorry, just afraid of getting in trouble. Dusa had a good mind to tell Teno and Yali everything Perse had said.

From the sea, a driving line of rain moved toward the island. From the sheltering bushes, Perse watched Dusa for a moment, then shrugged and ran toward a path so steep and dangerous that not even his father would have thought of using it.

Perse had no loyalty, Dusa decided. Teno was right, telling her not to make friends. Dusa was sorry she had gone looking for him, but Yali and Teno would not be pleased to hear that she had, and it would be better not to tell them.

She was still angry and frustrated when Yali called her for dinner, but mellowed as she dug in to delectable shish kebabs, lamb with orange segments, red pepper and onion, on a golden bed of fragrant saffron rice. "What are you planning next?" she finally asked.

Yali's eyes gleamed. "I've got a big surprise for you, Dusa. When Teno gets back from Athens, we're going on an archaeological cruise. How do you like *that* idea?"

Dusa stared at her. "I like it," she said slowly. "I like it, but it's very sudden. I need to get used to the idea. Are we going for sure?" she asked.

"We'll know tonight when Teno phones," replied Yali, "but I'm counting on it. The forecast looks good for the next week or more, and you've been working hard. We can all use a change of pace before cold weather sets in."

Dusa went up to her room. Snuggled in her cushions, she watched the waves far below. The setting sun threw a golden path across the sea.

The cruise sounded marvelous, but Dusa could not feel comfortable about it. At last, feet dragging, she went looking for Yali and found her at the computer in the office. A graphic of some kind was displayed on the huge monitor, something that wriggled. Dusa averted her eyes. "We've made a breakthrough in my treatment, haven't we," she said.

Yali swung the monitor so that the display was hidden. "Yes, indeed," she agreed, and waited, a question in her eyes.

"So," asked Dusa, "shouldn't we be going on with my therapy full-time? I mean," she floundered unhappily on, "I want to go on the cruise and all, but most of all I want to get better, Yali. I want to be cured."

Yali's solemn face split in a huge grin. Her tawny eyes gleamed. "Good girl," she said, "but you don't need to feel guilty. Teno called an hour ago, and she's done what she can in Athens. Your therapy will continue during the cruise. Indeed, I could say the cruise is the next step in your treatment. Does that put your conscience to rest?"

Dusa nodded eagerly, her own eyes catching fire in turn.

Yali went on, "Go and phone your mother. Explain that you won't be calling on Sunday, and maybe not next Sunday either."

Dusa had trouble talking to her mother again, but this time because she was thrilled, not because she was upset.

Pearl laughed. "Some therapy," she said. "Maybe I should look for a snake or two myself! Have a great time," she added, "I'll be thinking about you."

Dusa was first to hear the Cessna, toward noon the following day. She raced down the zigzag stairs.

Teno too seemed excited, tossing out supplies for Dusa and Yali to transfer to the boat.

What extraordinary supplies Teno had brought! Dusa recognized the scuba tanks, but there was other gear she couldn't even name, and rubber wetsuits, as well as a variety of fins, masks and snorkels.

"Yali, look at this," said Teno, handing a box up carefully. "It's an underwater light, a halogen rechargeable, the brightest I could buy." She stepped up to the dock. "Did you show Dusa around the boat yet?"

Yali grinned. "I waited for you," she said. "I get the impression she likes the idea of a cruise."

"What are we waiting for?" said Teno. "No time like the present." She ran lightly across the jetty and jumped down onto the deck. "Right this way, Dusa, come aboard."

What had happened to sedate, scholarly, reasonable Teno? This Teno was as volatile as a ten-year-old on the way to—what? a major-league ball game? Dusa laughed and skipped across the jetty herself. She loved boats, though the biggest one she knew was an elderly fourteen-foot sailing dinghy, property of the beach club on Lake Ontario, not far from home.

The cruiser was bigger than she had realized, compact but beautifully fitted. It had a vee berth forward, and a queen bedroom aft, a galley complete with microwave and fridge, even a handheld shower in the miniature bathroom. (Dusa knew enough boating language to call it the "head.")

When the gear and a lot of food had been stowed, Dusa, Yali and Teno settled themselves on the upholstered seats in the main cabin. Dusa goggled at the small TV. She could see a VCR player and a row of tapes. Forward, on a raised platform, the steering wheel was mounted, along with a formidable-looking instrument panel.

"How soon are we leaving?" Dusa asked.

Teno looked at her with darkly shining eyes. "Can we possibly leave tomorrow, Yali?"

"Maybe." Yali's eyes also glittered. "Tomorrow or the next day, for sure."

"How long will we be gone?" asked Dusa.

"As long as it takes." Teno squared her shoulders.

"What do you mean? As long as *what* takes?"

"As long as we want, I meant," Teno replied, with a sideways glance, oddly disconcerting. "Our tanks hold fuel for ten days' steady cruising."

Dusa had a sudden conviction that this trip was happening because of her. Was it possible? What had happened in that last hypnotic session?

Teno's voice broke into Dusa's racing mind. "Have you done any scuba, Dusa?"

"Scuba?" Dusa gulped. "No. There's a night course at school, but I'm too young to take it unless Mom came too. Anyway, I've been too sick."

"We'll help you," said Teno.

"You're not supposed to dive without taking a course," said Dusa doubtfully.

"It's part of your therapy," said Teno quietly, "and you'll be helping us at the same time. Indeed, Yali and I believe your role is crucial to our success. We'll make it safe for you."

Dusa smiled, eager to be convinced. That night, she packed her toiletries and a few clothes, including her three bathing suits. She was almost certain that Teno and Yali would be ready in the morning.

· · ·

The next day was glorious. Grabbing her bag, Dusa pelted down the circular stairs and ran out to the terrace. One look at Yali's glowing face was enough, but Yali confirmed the message with a laughing "yes." The cruiser bobbed cheerfully far below, calling Dusa to come aboard. Without even a thought of breakfast, she ran down the zigzag stairs, feet clanging on the metal treads.

Aboard the *Euryale*, Teno took the high captain's chair at the wheel and turned the key. The diesels started easily, then settled to a muted roar. Yali cast off, coiling the mooring lines neatly on the deck. She lifted huge fenders over the railing and stowed them in a locker at the stern. As this job was going on, Teno backed away from the pier, turned and headed out to sea.

Brilliant sun glinted on sapphire waves. Yali set out a chart, and Teno glanced at it casually from time to time, but she looked more often forward to the horizon, or back toward the island. Dusa had an odd feeling that either sister could have kept the boat perfectly on course even if she had been blindfolded.

The diving gear had been neatly packed into a wooden locker bolted to the open deck at the stern. Six scuba tanks were strapped upright on the starboard side. The diesels chugged on.

With no warning, Dusa felt snakes stirring in her head. "No," she cried out. "Go away, let me enjoy my cruise."

"Don't try to fight them," snapped Teno. "Dusa, here's a chance to be comfortable with your snakes even when you are not hypnotized. See if the little one will talk to you now."

Dusa rebelled. The snakes had been fairly amenable in the last few weeks. She had forgotten how they could take over, seizing both body and mind. Now they reminded her. In agony, she screamed, writhing on the floor.

Yali dropped to her knees and caught Dusa's body, pinning the girl's shoulders. "Don't fight them, Dusa," she too pleaded. "Let me try to find out what they need. Let me hypnotize you. Don't make this so hard for yourself."

In Dusa's head, the snakes set up a mad chorus of hisses. The wind rose and the cruiser rocked violently in the waves, creaking and groaning like a living creature amid the crashes and thumps of wind and sea. Teno held the wheel steady, shifting weight easily from one leg to the other.

Dusa watched with dull, incurious eyes. She did not want to be hypnotized. Even more, however, she did not want the agony of the snakes. At last she nodded. The snakes grew calmer immediately, as if this decision was exactly what they needed. Dusa was exhausted. As she listened to Yali's soothing voice, it was easy to let herself slip away.

Dusa had grown comfortable, mostly, with the little snake, her friend, her ally. This time, however, it was the great golden serpent that awoke, the biggest of all her snakes. In her trance, Dusa screamed in shocked surprise.

"Calm, Dusa, you are very calm," Yali's voice commanded. Dusa heard the voice from far away.

The great golden snake raised its head and turned this way and that, seeking. Like other snakes, its eyes were keen, and its sensitivity to odor was even more acute. Its forked tongue flicked in and out, picking up the distant, longed-for scent.

"Your right arm is very heavy." Yali's faint, insistent voice.

Dusa's arm was heavy as stone.

"Your arm is lifting. You are not lifting it, but it is lifting. Your finger is pointing, exactly the way we must go. Your finger is pointing, Dusa, pointing."

Dusa's stone arm lifted, pointing the way. Teno took compass bearings, made notes, and marked her chart. Hours went by. At last, in Dusa's head, the golden snake sank into peacefulness.

When she woke, Dusa did not know where she was or what she had been doing. Her watch said 10:15; the warm light filtering through the curtains said morning. How long had she slept? She was wearing pajamas, not her sleepshirt. A cozy comforter was tucked around her. Above her pillow, two walls came together in a sharp point. She was rocking, like a baby in a cradle. With that realization, her world slipped into focus.

She was in the small vee berth aboard Teno and Yali's cruiser, but there was no rumble of engines, only small slapping sounds of waves and an occasional gentle creak or thump or rattle from the boat. When Dusa pulled back the curtains, she saw the heavy anchor chain. It formed a taut line from the unseen winch above her to a point some distance in front of the cruiser where it vanished in the sea.

Her bladder was full to bursting. Dusa ran to the head, where she sat for a long time, dizzy and sick. The sick feeling passed, but when she stood up at last, she was still light-headed. Her mouth was dry, her stomach empty beyond hunger. Was it possible that she had slept through a night, a day, and a second night? Could she have lost more than twenty-four hours to hypnosis, or unconsciousness, or sleep? Absurd. She had missed her dinner the night before, that was all.

Climbing the stairs, Dusa heard laughter and excited voices. She found Teno and Yali at the stern, bent over the scuba gear. Both sisters stood up. Teno, still smiling broadly, set down a scarlet weight belt and weights.

"Have you had a good sleep?" she asked briskly, but she did not pause for an answer. "Are you starving? We've got a scuba lesson for you, it goes with breakfast. Come along."

Sitting at the mahogany gateleg table, Dusa ate scrambled eggs and toast and drank hot tea. Her dizziness disappeared with the first few mouthfuls of food. Yali started the tape: *Scuba Basics: A Review for Sports Divers*.

Dusa's eyes were turned toward the screen, but her mind was otherwise occupied. It was not fair that she had missed almost all of the outbound trip. No snakes, Dusa rashly promised herself, would keep her from enjoying the rest of the expedition. With this resolution and a third cup of tea, her frustration dissolved into warm contentment. The *Euryale* was an elegant boat. The table in front of her would be solid even in high waves, and it had an edge to keep dishes from falling off. She was going diving, and it would be perfectly safe. Yali and Teno would look after her.

Almost idly, Dusa began to pay attention to the video-tape. Again and again, the instructor said, "This is a review for certified divers. Nobody should try to dive without taking a proper course, part of it in a classroom and part in a pool." Embolism, decompression sickness—the more she watched, the more danger Dusa perceived. Did Teno and Yali really expect her to put on a tank and dive down to the ocean floor? She choked on her toast and jam.

When the tape was finished, Teno rewound it and started it again.

"I'm not doing this," Dusa announced at last. "It's crazy. Mom would kill me if I got drowned." She giggled nervously.

"This is part of your treatment," said Teno firmly. "We aren't showing the tape to scare you, just to give you a better idea of what you'll be doing. You'll be fine."

Teno took Dusa's arm and half led, half marched her to the stern. Both sisters soothed and reassured, but did not let go of Dusa as they eased her into a long-sleeved dive suit. The snakes were still, but Dusa could feel them, waiting. "Are you sure?" she quavered.

"Relax, Dusa," said Yali quietly. "Even if we didn't care about you, you're vital to our project. We have every reason to keep you safe. And we do care about you, Dusa, surely you know that. Teno and I are excellent divers, and we'll take total care of you. Nothing will go wrong."

Faced with so much conviction, Dusa felt the tension oozing out of her muscles. "Will I really be okay?"

"Absolutely," Yali replied. "Here, Dusa, try this mask." She held the mask to Dusa's face and waited for the girl to take a breath before dropping her hand. The seal was good, and the mask felt comfortable. Yali fitted a snorkel to the mask strap.

Dusa had snorkeled every summer at the beach club; that part would be easy. She bent to put on her fins. Everything felt unreal, including herself. It seemed she was about to take her first scuba dive.

"Tank and BC next," said Yali cheerfully. "Buoyancy compensator, Dusa. We'll adjust it for you. Now, stand on the platform. Teno, here's her weight belt." Their hands moved busily. "This is your regulator, Dusa. Air's on. Just breathe normally. Easy, isn't it."

In the heavy wetsuit, Dusa felt sweat running down her back, sweat gathering under her breasts.

Teno wore a shortie wetsuit. Quickly she buckled on her own tank and weight belt, then stooped with apparent ease to pick up a coil of rope and a long steel pole, perhaps an inch in diameter, with a pointed tip. A moment later, she stepped off the small platform at the end of the boat.

The splash brought a few welcome drops of water to Dusa's hot face.

Teno surfaced immediately and rocked in the morning's gentle waves. "Come on, Dusa," she called. "Hang on to your mask and regulator."

Dusa took a deep breath and counted: one, two, three. One huge stride, and she too was in the water. Adjusting her mask, she looked down.

Where she snorkeled, at home, the lake bottom oozed thick mud. No plants grew. The shell of a long-dead mussel poked up here and there, or an old tire, or maybe a pop can or white plastic cup. Here the ocean was probably deeper, but the water was clear. Dusa could see dark red and bright green marine plants below her, waving gently in the white sand. She thought she could see rocks. Suddenly she felt intensely happy. This was exactly what she wanted to do, more than anything else in the world.

Behind her there was another splash. Another masked diver, Yali, of course, swam in front of Dusa toward the anchor chain. She turned and beckoned. Dusa followed her. At once Teno was swimming at her side; the long pole gleamed. One after the other, holding the heavy chain, the three divers sank slowly feet-first through the water. As pressure built in Dusa's ears, Teno came beside her and pinched her nose, and Dusa remembered to blow out, hard. Her ears popped. Now she used her own hand, snorting as she went.

On the bottom, Dusa looked around in awed amazement. Little bright-colored fish darted here and there amid dark red sponges and purple sea fans. Yali and Teno wore only short wetsuits covering their torsos. Their bodies gleamed, almost like bronze. Dusa had not thought they were so deeply tanned. She heard a sound and looked up. Bubbles were rising from her tank. She must be hearing her own breath! She looked at Yali. No bubbles rose from her. Not from Teno either. Wildly, Dusa's head swiveled from one to the other. Suddenly her mask was full of water; her eyes were stinging and her vision blurred.

How could she clear her mask? It was easy, but Dusa

could not remember what to do. She could feel the snakes. She grabbed frantically at her mask, trying to pull it off, but found her arms held in a grip of steel. Without thinking, she started to inhale; suddenly, her nose was full of salt water. She swallowed convulsively, then gagged and would have spat the regulator out of her mouth if something—or somebody—had not prevented her. Somebody seemed to be willing her to breathe. To breathe out through her mouth. Out first, then in. Out and in.

Dusa exhaled. Inhaled. Great gasps of air, then slower.

The arms around her relaxed. A hand guided Dusa's hand to her mask. Now Dusa remembered how to clear it. You tipped your head back and tilted the bottom of the mask while you breathed out. She'd sat on the bottom of the lake and done it a hundred times. Lake water didn't sting, though.

Dusa cleared her mask. Almost all the water was gone. She could see. Teno floated beside her. Nervously, Dusa raised her eyes. A column of bubbles ascended from Teno's tank. Slowly Dusa turned to Yali. Bubbles there too. Everything was the way it should be. Yali joined thumb and forefinger in a circle. Now Dusa remembered and made the same sign herself. Okay, they told each other with their fingers, I'm okay.

In Dusa's head, the snakes murmured gently. She shivered, then moved forward, Teno and Yali gliding beside her. Soon Dusa stopped. Whatever the snakes wanted her to find, this was the place. She pointed downward, but Teno and Yali had already produced scrapers and begun to dig.

Brilliant green plants and mucky debris went tumbling.

Silt and sand rose. In the turbid water, Yali and Teno moved dimly, larger than life. Dusa suddenly felt cold. She backed away. How long had they all been down here? What if she ran out of air? How would she get back to the surface, to the boat? In sudden panic, she pushed off the bottom.

At once her ankles were seized and held. Heart pounding, she kicked frantically, but without the least success; her legs hardly moved. She sucked desperately on the regulator in her mouth, but nothing happened. She must be out of air! Now there was a masked face in front of her. Help! It was a silent scream. A pale finger tapped the regulator, then a second regulator appeared, snaking toward Dusa at the end of its black hose. She spat out the one in her mouth, seized the other, and gasped for air. Instead of air, however, she gulped a mouthful of salt water. Exhale first, dumbo, she reminded herself grimly. She coughed, sputtered, gasped again: air. Still not as much as her lungs craved, but she could breathe. The head in front of her nodded; a hand appeared in front of her eyes, forefinger and thumb meeting in a circle: are you okay?

Dusa found that she was becoming aware of herself again as a person, as distinct from an unthinking, panicked organism. Her heart no longer pounded. Her breathing had slowed, thought it was not yet calm and even. Now she could see that the masked figure facing her was Yali, and the regulator in her mouth was Yali's octopus: she was sharing Yali's air. Slowly she made her own okay signal, then pointed to the surface in mute appeal.

Yali pulled in her console and consulted her gauges,

then shook her head in a negative. She put an arm around the trembling girl and pushed off the bottom, but horizontally, not up. Dusa kicked languidly, but Yali's powerful legs moved them both efficiently, a few feet above the white sand, dark rocks and muck, and small green waving plants. Soon she stopped swimming and stood up, her arm still around Dusa's shoulder.

Teno lay prone in front of them, a knife of some sort in one bare hand and a stiff brush in the other. She was working at a long greyish rock, crusted with centuries of sea. Seaweed and broken shells went tumbling, along with bits of bright orange sponge. As Teno scraped and brushed, Dusa saw that it might not be a rock after all. Two stumps projected from the thing, curved toward each other. Could they have been part of a handle? In the museum Dusa had seen gigantic jars, taller than a person and far fatter. Could this possibly be an ancient pottery jar?

Looking at Teno, Yali let go of Dusa suddenly, and the girl lost her balance, jerking the regulator out of her mouth. Almost at once something pushed insistently against her lips. Yali was giving her a regulator; she pantomimed the action of breathing out. Dusa found herself breathing easily before she realized she was no longer using Yali's octopus. This regulator was attached to her own tank. By some miracle, it was giving her air.

Now things happened quickly. Yali hoisted the long steel pole. Teno took it and jabbed at the base of the long gray object. After several tries, she wedged the pointed end under the narrow part of the rock, or under the neck of the jar, if it was a jar. Yali made a noose at the end of her rope.

What could they be trying to do? Dusa watched as Yali joined Teno, and they pushed down on the far end of the pole. The gray object lifted with a sucking noise, then settled back again. Teno and Yali pushed the pole further underneath it. This time, their lever worked: the thing lifted out of the sand.

Yali looked directly at Dusa and motioned toward the rope, which wriggled a little with the slight movement of the water. Dusa shivered, feeling a sudden chill in spite of her rubber suit. The object lifted another few inches. Even though she was scared, Dusa bit back a giggle; the thing reminded her of a monster cookie jar, with stubby handles and a knobby lid. Yali wanted her to lasso it, no doubt. Dusa knelt awkwardly on the sand. Reluctantly, she picked up the rope and worked the noose over the lumpy stone. The jar-thing quivered as Dusa pulled the rope over the second projecting stump. She jerked her hands away just in time as the ponderous object settled again into the sand.

Yali and Teno had dropped the metal pole. Yali put her arms around Dusa and hugged her fiercely. Then she worked for a moment at the knot, apparently making the rope secure. She tied the free end around her own waist. Finally, she gestured upward. Teno and Yali each held one of Dusa's hands on the slow ascent. Dusa, looking up, saw their bubbles rising, three columns, small bubbles that grew bigger and bigger until they hit the surface and disappeared.

CHAPTER 8

B ack on board the *Euryale*, Yali untied the rope
from her waist and attached it to the swim platform.

"Lunch first," said Teno buoyantly, "and then up she
comes."

"Is that what you were looking for?" asked Dusa. "What
is it?" The snakes had nothing to do with it, she assured
herself. *How could I think they were showing me where to
go?*

"It seems to be an artifact of some kind," said Yali,
"very ancient, certainly. Yes, it is exactly what we were
looking for."

"That, and other things of the same kind," Teno added.
"You were wonderfully helpful, Dusa. You led us right to
it, even if you did not know what you were looking for. I
was sure we needed you underwater."

Dusa struggled with her wetsuit. Yali absently pulled the
jacket off her shoulders. After that, it was easier. Dusa was
extremely tired. She felt as if she had been underwater for

a lifetime, but in fact, if her bottom timer was right, the whole experience had taken only forty minutes.

Strange, what had happened with her tank. Why was she out of air, and then, after breathing from Yali's tank, okay again, getting air from her own regulator? Later, maybe she would ask. Or maybe not. Right now, Dusa did not want to know more about scuba.

Had there really been a period of several minutes when no air bubbles rose from Yali and Teno's mouths?

The snakes in Dusa's head were quiet. That gray thing, jar or whatever, had satisfied them. Nonsense! Insanity! Dusa knew the snakes had nothing to do with it.

Could that "artifact" be opened? Dusa had an irrational, macabre conviction that it could. Would Teno and Yali insist on opening it right away? She would not even ask. What stench of ancient decay might linger in its depths? What abomination might be hidden there?

After a quick lunch, Teno and Yali rigged a block and tackle. Dusa went to the vee berth, but could not sleep. She dozed off a time or two, but bumps and thuds from the deck roused her. Eventually she got up and parked herself on the stern deck to watch, her back against the cabin window, as far from Teno and Yali as she could manage in the confined space.

Teno was in and out of the water. Sometimes she seemed to be gone for several minutes, though she was not wearing a scuba tank. Of course Dusa could not see all the water surface; her vision was obscured by the boat, which was rocking much more than when they had returned from their dive. Teno must have surfaced several times where Dusa could not see her.

Yali pulled on the rope. Teno climbed over the stern rail to help her. Soon Dusa saw two white ropes, one at each end of a dark bulbous object. The object was clearly visible for a moment then disappeared again in the waves. However, there was no doubt that the treasure, whatever it might be, was coming to the surface.

Teno dived again into the water and brushed off more sand and silt. She guided the thing, seizing the right moment to push it onto the dive platform while Yali hauled on the ropes. The waves continued to grow higher, the wind noisier. The radio chattered urgently in Greek.

"Storm warning," said Teno angrily, as a furious gust slammed against the boat. The thing on the dive platform rocked and would have fallen if Teno had not moved with lightning speed; it rocked the other way and smashed against the stern rail. "Go to your cabin, Dusa, and stay there," Teno shouted. "Yali, we've got to get this thing on board."

"Can't I help?" yelled Dusa.

"No," barked Teno. "Get below, girl. Do as you're told," she snapped.

Words and tone left no room for argument, and Dusa moved fast. Out of the corner of her eye, she caught a flash of brilliance, but she did not stop to look. A minute or two later, she heard the winch and realized the anchor was coming up. One minute they tell you they can't do without you, she told herself, and the next they're yelling at you to get lost. She was still angry and frustrated when Yali called.

"Okay, Dusa," she said. "Come on up, it's all secure."

When Dusa entered the cabin, Teno had already started

the engines. She gave Dusa a quick, sharp glance. "You haven't done much boating," she said. "I should have briefed you. Look, Dusa, on any boat, the skipper is in charge. When I give an order, you obey. No questions, no discussion, definitely no argument. There isn't time. I have to depend on you, Dusa, and on Yali as well, or we could all be in trouble. Understand?"

Dusa nodded miserably. It was completely reasonable. Teno looked at her again. "It's not your fault, Dusa, don't feel bad about it. I can depend on you, can't I?"

Dusa nodded again. She felt ashamed that she had got in the way, and that she had been so angry. If she had thought, she could have understood without Teno's explanation.

Yali came in and flopped on a seat. It was the first time Dusa had seen her moving slowly and looking tired. A sudden violent squall brought rain drumming on the deck. The cruiser lurched drunkenly up the hills and down the valleys of the waves. Dusa sipped flat Coke through a straw from a covered glass. After one glance, she did not look outside. For a long time, she was sure she was going to be sick, but she was not. Nonetheless, she declined with a shudder when Yali suggested a sandwich. At last she staggered off to her cozy berth and fell asleep. She did not dream.

When Dusa wakened, the *Euryale* was chugging through placid seas under a brilliant sun. Teno looked as if she had not budged from the wheel. Yali moved about the tiny galley. Dusa smelled coffee and toast.

"Yum," she said. "I'm starving. Okay if I go up top after breakfast?"

"Sure," said Yali. "The warm weather won't last long. What do you call it? Indian summer?" Dusa nodded. "Take a towel to lie on. Catch some rays." Yali grinned, pleased with her own slang. "I found those tapes I told you about," she added, pointing to a hot pink plastic bag beside the television set.

Dusa ate quickly, then went back to her berth and slathered on sunscreen. She grabbed her Walkman and collected the bag of audiotapes on her way to the cabin door. Facing her on the rear deck, the artifact lay on its side, lashed against the gearbox. In that position the thing looked less like a jar and more like a rather dumpy sarcophagus, a version of the stone coffin in which ancient Egyptians buried their mummified dead.

Dusa turned her back on it and worked her way to the bow. She spread her towel and reached into the pink bag, wondering idly if any of the tapes would be worth listening to. Worth listening to! The plastic case in her hand held Bob Marley's *Legend*! Dusa goggled at it, openmouthed. Her favorite disc jockey back home had called it the greatest tape of modern times. How could the other girl have left it behind? Dusa scanned the label: "IS THIS LOVE?" "NO WOMAN NO CRY" "COULD YOU BE LOVED?" She sighed contentedly. Wherever that other girl was now, she must be kicking herself. Your loss, my gain, thought Dusa. She put the little plug in her ear and started the machine, waiting for the rich sound.

"Help me if you can," beseeched a voice in her right

ear. Dusa gaped at her Walkman. The spindles were turning; she could see the Marley label; the voice continued. "My name is Lucy Atherton. I'm in the north tower room at the Gordon Clinic. I've lived here for a year. I'm crazy most of the time. Maybe I'll be dead before anybody finds this tape. Help me if you can."

The tone changed suddenly, the voice turning sly, insinuating: "You help me, and I'll help you. Whoever you are, you need me as much as I need you." It changed again, now hard: "Don't tell them about this, don't you dare."

There was a long pause. Dusa, trembling, reached to turn off the machine. Her finger jerked away as the voice began again, a low, despairing cry: "What can I do? What can anybody do? Run for it, whoever you are. They're not Gordons." The voice laughed wildly here, but the laughter finally stopped abruptly and the voice went on.

"Gordon! Sure, sure, a typical Greek name! Use your eyes, and see what you see. Watch for two giant birds with gold-bronze scales and claws as sharp as razors—and human heads and women's breasts.

"They're monsters, right out of the old stories. Of course I'm crazy, that's why I'm here, snake-crazy, you can't believe a word I say. You can't believe they had a sister once, a murdered sister who had snakes instead of hair.

"It's no use trying to kill them, but you won't believe that either. I could get us out if I was well enough, I can fly that plane, but it's no good. You can't help me, nobody can help me. They're too strong.

"Save yourself, snake dreamer, run as far and as fast as you can. I know you're a snake dreamer, listening to this tape."

The voice changed again, pleading, lamenting, "I wish I could find it, oh I wish I could find it. My head hurts, I can't bear it. Stop them, stop the snakes."

There was a burst of horrid laughter, then a slight hissing sound. Was the tape really blank, Dusa wondered, or was she hearing the muted sound of Lucy's snakes?

In the bright sunlight, Dusa sat up, shuddering. She took the plug out of her ear and stopped the Walkman. She was sitting on a towel at the bow of a cruiser. Below her, two women kept the boat on course.

Monsters?

Impossible. The girl on the tape was totally crazy.

The north tower room would be above Teno and Yali's bedroom. The office–treatment room was on the ground floor below. She'd been there many times, but never heard a sound from above. Maybe a girl had once occupied that room, but she had gone home. Anything else verged on the territory of horror.

Dusa leaned forward and hugged her knees. What did she remember about that ancient story? They'd read it last year in English, and of course everybody had started calling her Medusa. How she loathed the name!

Once started, she remembered the story very well. Why not, in the circumstances?

Medusa the Gorgon had two sisters, Stheno and Euryale. (Oh boy, Teno and Yali. The *Euryale*. Dusa felt sick.) Perseus wanted to kill Medusa and bring back her head. This would be useful, because one sight of the snake-covered head was enough to turn a human being to stone. Dusa remembered how some kids had pretended to turn to stone when she came by. They'd stand on one foot or something until she turned her back, and then they'd laugh as if it was the funniest thing in the world.

Perseus borrowed all kinds of stuff from one god or another. Dusa had spoken up one day and said how unfair it was: Pluto's cap to make him invisible, Athene's mirror-bright shield so he wouldn't get turned to stone, Hermes' winged sandals so he could fly, and his sickle sword, whatever that was, to cut off Medusa's head.

Nobody helped Medusa.

Her snakes helped her, said one guy. Her head was covered with snakes and some of them always stayed awake so they could see anybody coming.

Snakes! Dusa said. Perseus had gods. It's not fair.

Medusa was a monster, said the teacher. She wasn't human.

It's always open season on monsters, I guess, said Dusa witheringly, and got sent to the office for talking back.

Perseus killed Medusa, of course, and put her head in a goatskin bag (another loan from Athene). He took out the head and used it whenever he wanted to turn anybody to stone. When he was finished with it, he gave it to Athene as a thank-you present for all the stuff she had lent him, and she put it on her shield and used it when she wanted to turn people to stone herself.

Nobody asked Medusa how she felt about it. Before Perseus came along, she was living with her sisters on a lonely island, keeping out of people's way. (What island would that be? Dusa didn't even want to think about it.)

Medusa was not killing anybody or hurting anybody. If anybody was a monster, it was Perseus.

Yesss, yesss, hissed the snakes in Dusa's head.

What was inside the object she had helped to raise from the ocean depths? Dusa gathered up Walkman, tape and towel. She crept back and swung herself down to look, really look, at the thing on the deck. It was a rock, nothing more, crusted with dying seaweed, broken shells and small sea sponges, once bright orange, now faded and drab.

But what a strange shape, for a rock! Dusa stared at the swelling belly of the thing, at the knobby end and the two crusted spheres, one on each side. She bent, then knelt, trying to see the underside. She rubbed off some gritty sand, then scraped with her fingernail. Surely no rock could be so smooth. Yali's amused, "Well, Dusa?" startled her, and she scrambled to her feet, blushing furiously.

"What are you thinking?" Yali asked.

Lucy's tape, the thing on the deck, Yali and Teno, who—what—were they? Dusa's mind was in a whirl. Desperately she hoped that Yali could not really see inside her head. The snakes stirred; Dusa could feel the little snake. To her amazement, she found herself becoming calm.

"What are you going to do with this thing?" she asked.

Yali patted the scabrous surface. "We'll study it," she said. "Teno and I take our archaeology seriously, even if we are amateurs. We'll take it back to the lab."

Dusa stared at her. Yali was still golden-eyed and slim. On board the cruiser she had been wearing jeans, but they were designer jeans—Pierre Cardin at the moment—and all her tops had logos. A Gorgon? Nonsense.

"Come on," said Yali. "Lunchtime."

Inside the cabin, Dusa stared at Teno, planted stolidly behind the wheel. Teno looked exactly the way she always looked: tailored navy pants, white shirt, short brown hair. The dark blue tie was loosened around her neck, the top button of the shirt undone. The navy blazer, neatly folded, lay across a padded seat. Teno's lips were their usual crimson.

For the first time, Dusa wondered if the dark red was really lipstick, as she'd thought, or if that carmine slash could be the actual color of Teno's lips. Of course, Teno's appearance might itself be the illusion, bronze scales and drooping breasts putting on the appearance of human flesh and clothes. And if you believe *that*, she told herself, and paused, at a loss for a completion that would express her scorn.

"Have you had a good enough look?" Teno's voice was dry. For a moment her keen eyes cut into Dusa's; then she turned forward again. Dusa was uncomfortably aware that Teno was still watching her, though not directly. "Well, Dusa, what is it?"

"Dusa is wondering about the jar, Teno." Yali smiled brightly.

Teno kept her hands steady on the wheel, but swiveled her head to study Dusa once more. The effect was disconcerting, almost as if the head was backward on the stocky body. "The jar," echoed Teno. "That's not surprising, considering your share in its recovery. What's on your mind?"

What could Dusa say? A voice on a tape? She could not betray Lucy's secret. "The snakes," she muttered. "I was looking at the thing, the jar, and I started thinking about

Medusa, I don't know why, we took it last year in English, and the snakes said yesssss." She felt tears forming, but they did not fall.

Teno nodded and turned her head once more back to its normal position, gazing through the window past the cruiser's bow to the expanse of ocean before them. The engines chugged, and they continued their steady way through the waves. Dusa had not seen land since the island had dropped out of view. Nobody spoke.

Eventually, without looking around, Teno said, "That seems perfectly reasonable to me. Why are you surprised? You are a snake dreamer, born of snake dreamers. Why would the snakes, the icons of your illness, not rouse themselves when you think of Medusa? She was the first snake dreamer of them all."

Dusa said desperately, "She wasn't real. My snakes are not real."

"What is real?" asked Teno. "That is as hard a question as 'What is truth?'" She paused. "Sorry, Dusa, that was a cheap shot. Let me try again. Your snakes are neither more nor are they less real than before, isn't that true?"

Dusa hesitated. "No," she said at last. "On the bottom of the ocean, I thought the snakes pushed me in one direction, and made me stop where I stopped. I've been telling myself ever since it didn't happen, but that's what I thought."

"Ah." Teno paused. "Do you still think the snakes did all that?"

"No," Dusa burst out, "it's impossible. Imaginary snakes could not do anything."

"True. Imaginary snakes could not. Yali, take the wheel." Teno sat down facing Dusa, staring into the girl's eyes.

"Go inside, Dusa," said Teno in her hypnotist's voice, low and strong, "go deep," and Dusa felt herself sliding. Something poked at her mind, a voice on a tape, a sense of danger, but it came too late. Dusa was already falling into the trance.

She sunned herself drowsily on a warm rock at the far end of the island. Her head was pillowed on her snakes. Most of the snakes were asleep, though you couldn't tell by looking at them; snakes have no eyelids to close.

There was a slight whirring sound, a little breeze on her cheeks. She opened her eyes lazily. The sun shone in a cloudless sky. Under and around her head, the snakes woke in sudden alarm.

Again she heard a whirr, louder. Something struck her neck, hard and sharp, and the snakes went crazy, and she screamed and screamed, watching blood spurt from her severed neck, watching her bloody head as it was stuffed into a big leather bag, and the snakes, writhing in pain but still struggling, were stuffed in on top.

Where were her sisters? She heard their screams, heard the beating of their great wings, but soon those sounds died away and she heard nothing at all. The silence went on and on. Her nostrils were full of the hot, rich smell of her own blood. She might close her eyes or open them; the darkness was no less. Slowly, she felt herself sinking toward nothingness. She would have been terrified if she had had energy for fear.

"Wake up, Dusa. Wake up. Wake up." The dreamer heard the repeated message, but faintly; the voice persisted for a long time, but it was very far away. Eventually, it faded.

In the bag, and also in Dusa's head, the little snake spoke clearly, and the dreamer repeated its words in English, translating the strange language without hesitation. "In me, victim and killer come together," Dusa said. "In my veins runs the blood of both."

Dusa heard herself speaking. She opened her eyes, and gazed into black darkness. Was she still in that dreadful bag? She screamed. A hand slapped her face. Dusa's shocked eyes focused on Teno, whose hand was raised for another slap. Dusa looked at Teno, then at the darkness, which she now saw clearly as the darkness of night through the cabin window. The room was never brightly lit when the boat was under way, but Dusa's eyes found and fixed on the dim overhead fixture with the same greedy thankfulness a parched wanderer in the desert might feel, coming upon a pool of water.

Teno and Yali stared at her. The wheel was untended, and the *Euryale*, steering herself, wallowed sluggishly in the waves. "You are back with us, Dusa." Teno breathed heavily, as if she had been running. "I am thankful."

"I remember my dream," said Dusa slowly. "I know everything that happened." She shuddered. One hand went automatically to massage her neck; the other clenched, as if to push away a leather bag.

Teno drew back abruptly. So did Yali. "We know your dream as well," said Teno. "You made it very clear."

"It was a dream, Dusa," Yali added firmly, "a fearful dream, but *not* part of your life."

The *Euryale* lurched. Both Teno and Yali jumped toward the wheel, Yali yielding to her sister. At once Teno pushed a lever forward; the engines roared, and the *Euryale* surged through the waves.

"Am I crazy?" asked Dusa helplessly.

"No, Dusa." Yali's voice was sharp. "You're exhausted. This was an important session for you, but we're all too tired to process it. Give it a rest. We found something important yesterday. Who knows, our discovery may change many things, for you as well as for us."

"I want to go home." Dusa blinked hard, holding back tears.

Lucy had begged for help, but Dusa couldn't help her and Lucy knew it, if she was still on the island. If Lucy wasn't crazy. If she was still alive. Dusa ached for her mother's arms around her, her mother sitting beside her on the couch, her mother singing her a lullaby as if she were still a baby, tucking her safe in her own familiar bed.

"I want to phone as soon as we get back and tell Mom I'm coming home."

"Of course you can phone as soon as we get back," said Yali. "We don't need to decide anything else tonight, do we? Come on, Dusa, I've made sandwiches and hot cocoa; then you must get to bed."

Dusa shivered in the vee berth, although she was wrapped in a down comforter. If there was a body without a head buried in the oak grove, could there be a head without a body in the gigantic jar? Madness!

A sentence from the television interview slunk into Dusa's mind and would not be dismissed. Had Yali said the words, or had Teno?

"For longer than you would credit, our dearest wish was to make our sister whole."

茴茴茴茴茴茴茴 〈HAPTER 9

Nobody said much the next morning. Teno and Yali took turns at the *Euryale*'s helm, maintaining speed. Dusa wondered again if she could have lost a whole day on the way out while she—or, rather, her great golden serpent—guided the *Euryale* to her destination. Surely the return trip was taking longer than it should. However, Dusa could not be certain of that.

How long had the boat been left to idle yesterday while she suffocated in that stinking bag? Afternoon had turned to night. Had the wheel been deserted for all those hours? She would not think about it. For certain, she would not ask. Dusa huddled with a book, or listened to her own tapes, and did her best not to think about anything else at all. The weather had changed; today, there was no warmth in the sun. When Dusa ventured out on deck, a chill wind whipped at her hair. It was a relief when she sighted the high black cliffs of the island, dead ahead.

They docked about noon. "Go on up, Dusa," said Yali.

"Lunch should be ready in half, three-quarters of an hour. If we're not there, you go ahead and eat."

On the pier, Dusa felt the ground moving under her, as if she were still on the cruiser. She staggered up the zigzag stairs, was relieved to find the front door unlocked, and did not stop until she flopped on her bed in the tower room.

When she came down to the terrace, she was ravenous. Yali had set out dark bread, slices of cold veal and a bowl of tabouli salad, along with tomatoes in wedges and two dishes of green olives, one hot and spicy, the other mild. Dusa piled her plate with food and filled her glass with diet Coke.

Food has been known to bring on visions. If Teno and Yali were monsters, the food they gave Dusa might foster the illusion that they were human. Dusa put down her fork. Perhaps she should stop eating entirely. The mint-parsley-lemon smell of the tabouli teased her nostrils. She starved herself for five minutes, timing them on her watch, before snatching up the fork once more.

Teno and Yali were nowhere to be seen. Would they appear on the terrace with bronze-gold scales and dragon wings? Dusa was relieved but not really surprised when they came in looking much as usual. Teno had exchanged her navy skirt for pants in Athens, but had not varied that attire, except for swimming and the scuba dive, since they arrived on the island. Today once again her costume was unchanged, her mouth still a crimson slash.

Yali had worn designer jeans on the boat. Today she wore the jungle print pantsuit in which Dusa had first seen her. Maybe no detail of their appearance was real, Dusa reflected. Perhaps it was all done by hypnosis. If so, they were powerful indeed: her mother, the television interviewer and presumably the entire audience back home had seen them in the same disguise.

Dusa had been impressed by Yali's designer chic right from the start. Like most girls who are not fashion models, she had wondered, in an admiring kind of way, how Yali could possibly manage to keep looking so fabulous. Now, for the first time, she questioned how in real time that bandbox look could be created and maintained.

Yali had no hairdresser, no laundress, no access to a dry cleaning establishment, let alone a high-fashion boutique. Despite that, everything she wore looked brand-new. If she spent hours doing her own hair and makeup, Dusa did not know where those hours came from. Yali had little enough time for sleep. (If she was a monster, however, perhaps she had no need of sleep. Dusa pondered. In the old story, Medusa's sisters were asleep when Perseus arrived. What did that prove? They could sleep if they wanted to. It didn't prove the need.)

Conflicting realities warred in Dusa's head. In one universe, she (patient, here to be cured) sat at lunch with two expert therapists, dedicated to making her well. If beautiful surroundings contribute to good health, they could not have chosen better. Dusa gazed out at an immensity of cloudless deep blue autumn sky and velvet sea. In the serene height of the terrace, calmness flowed in, agitation receded. If Dusa did not let her mind loose, this place was clearly part of the known world: the twin-towered mansion behind her, the stone-floored patio where they sat, the planted terraces and the sunlit ocean glittering far below. In another part of that same world, her mother was waiting.

Part of Dusa wanted desperately to see no more than that, to dismiss everything else.

Too much, however, failed to fit: the clinic with no patients, the tombstone in the oak grove, the scuba expedition and the ancient jar (Dusa could see it, diminished by distance but clearly visible on the deck of the cruiser at the pier below), glimpses of two great bronze creatures, Lucy's cry for help, and above all, the snakes and her own strange dreams. Serenity was an illusion, the more dangerous because the feeling was so strong.

For a fleeting moment, Dusa wondered if she was so crazy that she was inventing all the anxiety-producing events. Perhaps her eyes and ears were no more to be trusted than her mind. At this thought, her rage swelled. I am not crazy, she told herself firmly. I have seen what I have seen. I have felt what I have felt.

If Dusa was not crazy, then Teno and Yali would be busy in some highly unusual ways. First, they had to open the object they had raised. If they found what they wanted and seemed to expect, then they would have to dig up something under or near the coffin stone. Dusa told herself to stop ducking away from the words: if they found their sister's head, then they would have to dig up her body. Then, presumably, they would put the two together and bury—or try to resuscitate—snake-haired Medusa, whose glance turned people to stone.

Put that way, the whole idea was ridiculous: Frankenstein territory. Dusa wished she could laugh at the image she had conjured up. If her mother were here they would laugh together.

Yali's voice broke into the girl's absorption. "We're going to the boat," Yali said. Her voice fell into the low, compelling tones of hynotherapy. "Go to your room, Dusa, you're very tired, you need rest. Have a nice warm bath and then go right to bed."

Dusa nodded obediently and turned away. She could almost feel herself sinking into the Jacuzzi, rousing just enough to towel off before falling into bed. As she walked along the corridor to the breakfast room and the circular stairs, however, Lucy's voice echoed in her mind: "Help me if you can."

Dusa shook off the hypnotic drowsiness, forcing her feet to move briskly. She ran up to her own bright room and crossed to the windows, craning forward to see the zigzag steps against the cliff. She had expected to see Yali and Teno still on the way down, but there was no sign of them. Odd. Even at a fast run, they could not possibly have reached the bottom so soon. Dusa opened a central window and leaned out. Two small figures, far below, were climbing into the boat.

How could they move so fast? Now Dusa's adrenaline was pumping. She ran downstairs again, back through the house to the office on the ground floor of the north tower. The telephone sat on a corner of the huge glass-topped desk. Dusa picked up the receiver hopefully, but the machine was dead. Had it gone down in the storm? How did it work? By radio? By satellite? Knobs and buttons did not tell her. She tried pushing a few of them, almost at random, although with little hope of success. She needed calmness and time to think, and at the moment she had neither. She was afraid to experiment much with the apparatus; Yali and Teno must not know she had been here. She ran out to the foyer and tried the phone there with no better success, then ran back again to the office.

Two black four-drawer horizontal file cabinets stood against the wall behind the desk. Not surprisingly, they were locked. Dusa opened the top drawers of the desk and felt in the corners, hoping to find keys. No such luck. She made a face, then bent to look carefully at one of the locks. This file cabinet was obviously expensive, but the lock looked no different from her mom's cheapie at home, and Dusa knew exactly how to release the metal locking rod on that one. A steel ruler would do it—and she had just seen one in the desk! A minute later, the top drawer of the black cabinet slid toward her. At once Dusa wanted to look at her own file. Now, however, her business was with Lucy Atherton. Her own record would have to wait.

Each olive-green folder in the crowded row was neatly labeled: Abalos, Antonia; Abbas, Mirza; Abdi, Maryann; Abel, Renée. Dusa's eyes skipped impatiently along the row. And these were only the As! Allen, Sandra; Ambeau, Charlene; Arch, Josepha.

There it was: Atherton, Lucy, almost at the end of the row. Dusa pushed the other folders away, making space to open the one she wanted.

It couldn't be empty.

But it was. Disappointment swept through her. She wriggled the folder out of the drawer, as if it were bound to acquire some contents on the way to the desk, but when she put it down, it was empty still.

Could Lucy's records be misfiled? Quickly Dusa explored Athanasios, Georgia, and Atkinson, Mary, on each side of the folder she had removed. Georgia's file smelled musty. No wonder; she had been admitted in 1905, discharged in 1906. Impossible. Teno and Yali weren't that old!

Dusa shook herself. How could anyone get used to such a story? If a person was going to believe it, Teno and Yali were hundreds, no, thousands of years old. 1906? Surely she had misread the file, and the right date was 1960. All the same, Dusa did not look again. Mary's stay was much more recent: 1987 to 1990. There was nothing about Lucy Atherton. Except for her name on a folder, and a voice on a tape, there was nothing to show that such a person had ever existed.

Dusa eyed the stairs, then looked down at her faithful Timex. It was an analog sports model, an anachronism in a digital age, but her mother had given it to her and Dusa loved it. She had meant to set the bezel to the time she began her search, but, looking down, knew she had forgotten. How long had Teno and Yali been gone? Twenty minutes? Half an hour? She spun the bezel carefully, setting it for the longer time. Did she dare look out of the window once more? Could she possibly be in danger from something that had lain at the bottom of the sea, perhaps for more than two thousand years? The snakes were still active, it seemed. Medusa's head, if it existed, might still have power. Dusa did not look out.

She ran to the staircase and up to the next floor. Teno and Yali's bedroom was the mirror image of her own at the other end of the house. Instead of cushioned window seats, however, the windows were lined with low wooden stools, richly carved. Woven mats glowed in jewel colors on the stools, larger mats on the polished floor. The bed was round, lower and larger than Dusa's, a vast circle piled with cushions. Dusa walked over and looked down. On one cushion, a hoofed hairy creature, human from the waist up, played a set of pipes. On another, a naked woman, long fair curls cascading over tip-tilted breasts, took an apple of gold from a man who knelt at her feet.

Dusa wrenched her eyes away. There was no filing cabinet to be seen, and no headboard where files might be concealed. A massive wardrobe, even bigger than the one in her own room, glowed with pale circles of mother-of-pearl inlay and with squares of shining blue. Dusa pried and poked, breaking a fingernail. She could not find a door, let alone a lock and key to the huge piece, which might not be a wardrobe after all.

The room's high ceiling was plastered and painted white. Track lighting ran around the edge. As far as the ceiling was concerned, this might as well be a room in a modern house. It was not modern, though. Dusa knew in her bones that this structure was centuries old. The iron staircase, twin of her own, spiraled up. Where her room was open to the next floor, however, here the stairs ended abruptly, butted against a trapdoor.

Dusa gathered her courage and went up the stairs quickly. The trapdoor above her head was painted to match the rest of the ceiling, but it was boxed in and secured by a hasp and a padlock of heavy bronze. No steel ruler would release that lock!

Dusa pelted down the two flights of stairs and ran to the big pedestal desk. Might not the keys be here after all? Frantic now, Dusa pulled out the center drawer, almost spilling its mixture of pens, paper clips and other office supplies on the floor. Again she felt in corners, lifted boxes. Nothing. Dusa pushed that drawer shut, then began on the others, repeating her wild search. The sixth drawer brought success: her fingers closed on a small ring of keys.

Dusa ran upstairs again, trying one key after another. Frantically she poked and pushed, but to no avail. No key on the ring would enter the bronze lock. The room above defied her.

Dusa was suddenly drained of energy. What could she hope to do, all by herself, against two creatures who perhaps had lived forever, whose powers she could only guess at? She crept over to the window and looked down.

The sky had darkened; another storm was moving in. Far below, two gleaming figures seemed to bend over the long gray jar, which now lay on the pier. A jagged fork of lightning split the dark sky, drawing Dusa's gaze. Thunder rumbled. She had not counted the seconds, but the lightning could not be far away. Dusa looked back at the scene below. In the moment when her eyes had been averted, the gray shape had split like an oyster. Above one open half-shell, two gleaming figures leaned toward each other, dark head meeting fair.

What were they looking at? Dusa drew back. If it was in

fact the fantastic object that her mind visualized, she dared not look, even at that distance.

The first large drops of rain splattered against the windows. The room was now very dark, but any light would betray her presence there. Dusa hoped the desk drawers would not show that she had ransacked them.

As she watched, Teno's navy-suited figure appeared at the top of the cliff, followed by Yali. Both sisters looked dry, as if they had stepped outside that very minute, though the rain immediately beat against them. Dusa watched while the jungle print pantsuit plastered itself against Yali's slim body. A beautiful body. Dusa admired it, not for the first time. Human, female human, no doubt about it. What was all this nonsense about Gorgons?

Then Dusa saw the bag that Teno carried, cradled in her arms. In blind panic, she ran for the shelter of her room.

◪◪◪◪◪◪◪ CHAPTER 10

Dinner that evening was a distant meal. Nobody seemed much interested in talk. Even if they had been, the rain, crashing against the windows, would have made conversation difficult.

"Did you sleep this afternoon?" asked Teno. "Are you feeling better?" Dusa nodded quickly, dropping her eyes. She was hungry again, and the souvlaki, four skewers nestled in a bed of rice, was wonderful. Again she wondered if the food fostered illusion. She put down one chocolate brownie, then reached for two, hiding the second one in the kangaroo pocket of her old red sweatshirt.

"Why not phone your mother?" suggested Yali. "You seem calmer, Dusa. I hope you've changed your mind about rushing home."

Dusa nodded. No doubt the phone was working now. The panic had left her, and her curiosity was stirred. Besides, she could not leave without some response to Lucy's appeal. "I don't even know what day of the week it is," she said.

"Friday," said Yali. "If you call the office, you'll likely reach your mother before lunch."

Dusa used the phone in the foyer. Pearl was with Mr. Sanderson at a client's office and would not be back that day. Dusa left a message of love and returned to the dinner table.

Teno turned searching eyes on the dark-haired girl. "Dusa, we're putting the lab off limits to you," she said evenly. "We'll be there often, starting tonight, but the door will be locked. This is for your own safety. There may be some risk in the material we've found; we cannot allow you to be exposed. Also, the material will certainly be fragile; we must work in a controlled environment. Am I making sense?"

Dusa nodded. "Will you tell me about it?" she asked.

"Sure, when we find anything interesting. It may take a while."

"Will you let me see what you're doing? When you're sure it's safe?"

"Yes," said Teno.

Dusa loaded the dinner dishes onto a cart, which she wheeled out to the kitchen. Not long after she arrived, Dusa had begun to help with the evening cleanup, and soon she had fallen into a pattern of doing the job alone. Teno did not suggest that this was work for Dictys and Perse. She and Yali were obviously pleased to get rid of the chore, and Dusa was not unhappy to take it on. The kitchen, with its six-burner gas range, walk-in freezer, and oversized dishwasher, had become familiar. Where in it might she find a small bronze key?

She rinsed the dishes and stacked the dishwasher.

There was a key rack beside the back door. It seemed unlikely that the key she wanted would be displayed in plain sight, but Dusa looked just the same.

Keys for the plane and the cruiser were labeled, as well as keys for the house doors. A large padlock hung with its keys on a hook. There was no bronze key, even when she took the rack down and looked behind it, no key that looked to Dusa as if it might possibly fit the padlock in the ceiling.

If Yali and Teno seldom went into the tower room, the key could be anywhere. It could even be lost. If that room was in use, however, a key must be somewhere in easy reach. It could be on either sister's key ring, of course, along with duplicates to some of the other keys Dusa had found. Teno had used keys on a ring to start the boat and the plane. Other keys had also dangled from the ring.

Dusa did not have time to make a complete search. Her mind made fearful pictures of the lab, with Yali and Teno, bird-footed and glittering, crooning softly to a gory, snake-covered head. Crazy. What if she got into the tower room and found nothing? There was no Lucy. But what if there were?

Yali and Teno had not forbidden Dusa to go to the boat. She had seen a small toolbox there with a hammer, a bunch of screwdrivers, and various other hand tools.

The cold wind beat against Dusa on the zigzag stairs, and she held the railing compulsively, but the rain had almost stopped and her rubber-soled shoes did not slip on the wet metal treads. In the soft dusk, some of the terror left her, even though the stairs seemed so unsubstantial. Descending, she seemed to hover between earth and sea.

On the pier, the thing they had raised lay, split long-ways, looking now like a great gray peapod with a keyhole end. The inside of both halves was black with something that might be tar. Dusa took a deep breath and began to edge past the ugly thing. She hopped down to the boat. A gust of wind blew across the pier and a faint breath of ancient stench hit her nostrils, bringing a nightmare memory of rotting leather soaked in blood. Dusa exhaled frantically, then held her nose.

Inside the cabin, the air was untainted. Dusa found the switch for a dim cabin light. She took several shuddering breaths before kneeling to slide back a panel under the seat. The red toolbox, that sane ordinary thing, was exactly where she remembered it. Hammer, screwdrivers and other oddments were there, a small oilcan, an assortment of broken washers and rusty screws, a box of tarnished brass screws and fittings.

Dusa took out the hammer and several screwdrivers, hesitated, then put them back, closed the lid and picked up the whole box, turning off the light. Toolbox in hand, she edged once more past the gray shape. The pier was unlighted, and Dusa imagined stumbling, falling into stinking blackness, but she did not fall. In the gathering darkness, she fled shivering up the stairs.

What if Teno and Yali had left the lab? They'd see her with the red toolbox. What would she say? Luck was with her, however. The huge central living room, when she reached it, was empty; so was the breakfast room next door. Dusa did not take the toolbox to her bedroom; the circular mirror hovered there, ready to betray her to a distant watcher via a television monitor. She hid the box behind the living room cushions in the window seat.

What next? Dusa was still shivering. She took a Hershey bar and a glass of milk with her and dragged her weary self upstairs to her room.

Breakfast might have seemed as quiet a meal as dinner the night before. However, the air around the three diners was tense.

Teno had changed her navy tie for a carmine one that matched her lipstick. Against her white shirt and tailored navy jacket, the crimson flared like a banner.

Yali's designer outfit was the wildest Dusa had seen: shimmering gold and silver lamé, low cut and revealing, hugged Yali's slim body. Diamonds cascaded from her delicate ears. High-heeled silver sandals completed an outfit that would have graced the most formal occasion but which seemed wildly out of place at the glass-topped wicker table.

"Where's the party?" The question popped out before Dusa took time to think.

A slow smile rose to Yali's lips. "Do you like my outfit?" she asked.

"I like all your outfits," said Dusa. "They suit you perfectly."

Yali nodded. "This material is unique," she said.

Dusa looked in confusion at Yali's tunic top.

"No," smiled Yali, "I don't mean this fabric, I mean the stuff we found. It is thrilling. We need to work on it full time for the next week or so. Can we persuade you to take a break from therapy? We think it will be good for you, give you time to integrate what we've done so far."

"Sure, I guess."

"We must collect samples for pollen counts around the island," said Teno. "We'll need soil samples as well. Can you find enough to do today? Swim if you like. The water will be warmer than the air, and you've got your wetsuit. Just don't go out too far."

"Can't I . . . ?" Can't I help you, Dusa had been about to ask, thinking of pollen counts and soil samples, and the fun of clambering about the island, the satisfaction of helping. How easy it was to forget about that tape, to ignore all the oddities, to act as if nothing unusual had happened at all.

"Can't you what?"

"I want to phone Mom," said Dusa.

"Now? It's two A.M. in Toronto," said Teno. "Anyway, I'm afraid you're out of luck. You got through yesterday, I know, but now the phone is completely out of action. The storm damaged our radio relay and some other electrical equipment. We need a new transformer and some parts for the generator. I'll have to go to the mainland before long."

"When?" asked Dusa. Her voice quivered, despite her efforts to keep it steady.

"Soon," Teno replied. "But things here won't wait; we need to stabilize the material we found and begin to work with it. Your mom won't worry. She knows the phone is not completely reliable. I got cut off one night myself, talking to her."

154

"Go for a swim," said Yali kindly. "Take your mask and snorkel and watch the fish. Or lie out on the terrace with your music tapes. Dictate some of your snake dreams."

Look for Perse, thought Dusa, or for his father. They had helped the others to get away. Dictys had not wanted to help, though, Dusa remembered, and Yali and Teno had been on another continent at the time. "Do my dreams still matter?" she asked.

"Certainly," replied Yali in a soothing tone.

In Dusa's head, the little snake stirred. There seemed to be a question, or perhaps a warning, in its hiss. Dusa tensed. At once, the little snake subsided. In her mind, it had felt friendly, concerned for her. Dusa blinked. Yali and Teno were talking to each other, as if Dusa was not there.

The situation still seemed unreal, but it was a dream from which Dusa could not force herself to wake. She looked at Teno, solid in her navy suit, and Yali, more ethereal but equally solid in her shimmering outfit, and tried to see through those physical forms and visualize bronze scales, bright wings, snaky heads and naked women's breasts. Monsters as old as time, the third one in pieces, to be put back together perhaps into some horrid kind of life? A head that turned human beings to stone with a single glance? If the scene in front of her was difficult to accept, that alternate reality was totally impossible.

Yali interrupted her reverie. "What are you thinking?"

Dusa shook her head, trying to clear her mind. She shrugged. "Nothing." She could not see them as different creatures or inhuman. She might behave as if the bronze scales and all the rest were real, as if there was a real body to be rescued, a real and deadly head, but she could not bring herself to believe it.

"We'll get on, then," said Teno. "We'll be starting in the lab."

"Don't forget to lock it," said Dusa politely.

Teno smiled and nodded. "Right, see you later."

It was easier, though not a lot easier, for Dusa to accept the nightmare possibility after Yali and Teno were no longer sitting in front of her. The body was buried in the oak grove. Yali and Teno would have to go there. Unburying the body—exhuming it, that was the word—would take a while. When they went to the oak grove, she would break into the tower room. Then it would be time to look for Perse.

Dusa went to the kitchen. Even though she had just finished breakfast, she felt hungry. Absently, she made herself a double-decker peanut butter and honey sandwich and poured a glass of milk. Bronze peanut butter, deep gold butter, pale gold honey, was all of it food to fuel bronze-gold visions? Monsters or not, Teno and Yali kept a well-stocked kitchen. If she did at last escape from the island, she would not starve on the way.

Escape? The thought had not entered Dusa's mind before. Now, suddenly, it seemed possible that Yali and Teno might not intend to send her home. "Help me if you can," the girl on the tape had said.

"Yessss," hissed the voices in her head.

Dusa shivered. A month ago, she would never in the world have believed that she would want to welcome the snakes, her snakes. She had left Pearl and come to this island for no other reason than to be rid of them. Now, in blinding realization, Dusa knew they were her only hope.

On the boat, after Teno and Yali had brought up the jar, Yali had said, "Our discovery may change many things, for you as well as for us." One change had been immediate: now Dusa understood the language of the snakes and knew more of their power. She put her hands on her thighs, the way she did in the hypnotic sessions, and leaned back as best she could in the straight wooden kitchen chair.

"Help me, my snakes." She focused inward, letting herself sink deep, "Help me, my little snake."

"Yessss. Lissten."

Now Dusa could hear other voices, familiar somehow, and the strange language was familiar as well. Dusa listened, not with her own ears, but with the keen hearing of the little snake; the language might have been her mother tongue.

"Dear heart, come back to us," one voice entreated. "The pain is over, dear one, let yourself come back."

"Say something," purred another voice. "Dear one, speak to us." There was a pause.

"That snake moved!" the first voice was sharp. "The little one. There!"

"I didn't see it."

"No matter," said the first voice. "No rush. Dear one, let yourself come back."

"Should we get the girl?" asked the other, Teno probably, though Teno's voice had never sounded so tender. "Is that the energy you need?"

Dusa's muscles tightened in sudden shock, and the

snake was gone, the contact was gone, there was nothing to hear. The door screeched. Dusa jumped, and her glass of milk went flying.

"What's wrong?" Teno demanded brusquely.

"I want to go home," said Dusa, and burst into tears.

Teno looked at her impatiently. "Don't be a nuisance, Dusa," she said. "We're going to get soil samples and things. Settle down. Go for a swim."

"We'll be back later," added Yali.

"Stop crying, Dusa," Teno continued with irritation, "you're not a baby. And remember, stay away from the lab."

The kitchen door swung closed behind them, and a moment later Dusa heard the softer sound of the front door. She gulped and snuffled, took a deep breath and wiped her eyes. The sudden tears had surprised her as much as they apparently surprised the other two. Dusa went to the far window to see if the two figures were heading, as expected, toward the oak grove. Far below, something gleamed for a brilliant moment before vanishing into the trees.

Back in Toronto, Pearl Thrasman slept uneasily. It was too bad that the telephone at the clinic was so unreliable; unreasonable too, in this age of satellites. Dusa was back on the island after the cruise, but Pearl had phoned again and again since getting her daughter's message without getting through. She'd called herself a fool for worrying, and worried, if anything, even more. "I don't like it," Dr. Andrews had said, when she had telephoned him.

At last Pearl had called the Canadian embassy in Athens, and a courteous young man had promised to make inquiries, although he expected it might take a day or two.

Though it was very early, Pearl wakened at the telephone's first ring; she clutched the instrument. "Dusa?"

"No, Mrs. Thrasman. My name is Diana Christopolis. I apologize for telephoning you at this hour. Mr. Barakos at your embassy thought you would want to talk to me. From what he told me, I knew I should not wait."

🬀🬀🬀🬀🬀🬀🬀 CHAPTER 11

D usa sat on the cushions as if paralyzed, staring at the
trees where the gleam of gold had disappeared. At
last she summoned will and energy. The little toolbox still lay under the cushions, near the stairs that curved
on and up to the tower room. Now that she had snapped
out of her lassitude, the tower room again beckoned, more
urgently than before.

She grabbed the red metal box and ran across the office,
up through the bedroom to the trapdoor where once more
the bronze padlock and plated hasp forced her to stop. Her
heart pounded; she could hear the thump, thump of her
pulse. With a shaking hand she opened the little red box
and took out the screwdriver. She wanted the room to be
empty. She longed to believe in Teno and Yali.

Dusa knew how to install a hasp so that the top part
would fit over the bottom and cover the screws. "Lots of
people put them on wrong way round," Granddad had
told her, long ago. "Anybody with a screwdriver can take
off the hasp and the padlock too. Easy." Dusa had hoped

this hasp would be that easy. No such luck. The top was bent back, neatly hiding the screws underneath.

Dusa inserted her screwdriver into the space between the top and bottom of the hasp and pulled down. If she could not bend the hasp, she would try to loosen the screws, using the screwdriver as a lever between them and the wooden joist. She pulled and twisted, then gave a sudden jerk. Again. The metal bent slightly.

Dusa jerked at it desperately. The screws held, but the hasp bent more and more. Now Dusa pawed through the toolbox, looking for a screwdriver with a right-angled handle. Would this small toolbox contain such a thing? She couldn't find it, but a stubby-handled screwdriver jumped into her hand. Hasp and screws were shiny and new. The screws would not be rusted into the wood. Dusa caught the edge of a slotted screw and twisted. The short screwdriver slipped in her sweaty hands. She wiped them on her shirt, then twisted again. Her hands ached. With a long screech, the first screw began to turn.

The other screws were easier. Soon the hasp hung free.

Nervously, Dusa pushed up the trapdoor. It moved easily on hinges that were, like the hasp, shining and new. Why would anybody take all this trouble for nothing? On the other hand, maybe something important had been here but wasn't any more. Dusa found a latch and used it to hold the door open. She touched her forehead for luck ("Hard wood's best!") and hoped the room was empty. Up she came.

Disappointment hit her like a blow. Dusa faced a hospital room, though the medical gear looked out of place here, where the circular walls rose only three or four feet before tapering to a cone. This space was the twin of the tower room above her bedroom, Dusa realized, but it seemed bigger, barer, lonelier.

A high bed with bars on each side stood in the middle of the floor. It looked empty. Dusa tiptoed toward it. The area was brightly lit by a circle of halogen lights. On one side of the bed, a bank of electronic instruments hummed. Green zigzags danced across a monitor screen. An IV stand, with bag and tubes, stood beside the bed.

The bed was not empty. The white woven coverlet was raised in the middle. Dusa took the last few steps quickly and stood frozen, unable to look down. What did she expect? It could be anything, something monstrous, something that would change her forever. Snakes, perhaps. Stone, or something that would turn her to stone. Dusa laughed hysterically, raising her level of terror another notch. She twitched aside the coverlet.

Dusa shuddered. Could this be the girl who had made the tape? This creature would never pilot a plane. It was only a guess that the lank form was female, something in the hair, more than the face itself. The face was gaunt, skeletal, with colorless skin pulled tight over high cheekbones, and a long, sharply pointed chin. Drab blond hair was combed severely back and braided, one braid over each shoulder.

Was she alive? The line on the monitor zigzagged across the screen. The IV tube was taped to a hand almost as white as the coverlet. Looking, Dusa could see no motion suggesting breath. The coverlet was still.

Who was this creature? What did it mean, finding her here? Yali and Teno had lied, that was all. One patient had not been cured. Even if this was Lucy, that did not make Teno and Yali Gorgons.

Dusa licked her finger and held it under the waxy nostrils. Did she feel a slight stir of air, a tiny coolness? She could not tell.

"Lucy," she hissed, then louder and more urgently, "Wake up, Lucy. Talk to me."

Translucent eyelids stirred as if they would open, then relaxed again. "Lucy!" Dusa's hand closed on a bony shoulder.

The face she was watching contorted in terror. High animal screams broke from the frenzied mouth. "Hush, Lucy, hush," whispered Dusa. In panic, she scrabbled at the high railing by the side of the bed. At last the barrier dropped with a clang, and Dusa reached for the emaciated body. She found herself cuddling a skeleton, repelled and at the same time terrified of damaging the bony thing. However, Dusa knew those screams, that writhing. Again and again, Pearl had held her just as she held this creature. She rocked and sang, "There, there, you're safe with me," finding a rhythm and a two-note tune for the words, which she repeated again and again.

The screams gradually subsided, and the writhing body grew quiet. Lucy—if this was Lucy—gulped and gasped for air. At last the pale eyelids fluttered open, and Dusa looked anxiously down into light blue eyes, faded, like everything else about this girl.

"Lucy?" Dusa tried once more, and felt the head nod against her. "Don't try to talk. You're tired. I know all about it. My name is Dusa. I'm a friend." Joy washed over Dusa in a sudden wave. She had found a friend!

"You need energy," Dusa said at last. "There's juice in the fridge. I'm going to the kitchen, Lucy. I'll be right back."

Lucy's right hand tightened on Dusa's arm. The bony head shook in a negative.

"I have to," protested Dusa. "One minute? Two? Yali and Teno are out. Lucy, I'll be right back." As she looked down, however, her euphoria faded. This skinny creature seemed sick to death. What if she died? Oh, if only Dusa could turn the clock back, an hour, even forty minutes, she could climb back down the stairs, leaving the hasp untouched, and never have entered the tower room at all.

Lucy's eyes went to the front window. Urgently.

"What?" asked Dusa. She went to look. A large, curved section of window was unlatched and partly open. Dusa latched it, then locked it, though unsure why she bothered. What was the danger in an open window? Did Lucy expect two bronze creatures to fly into the room? Crazy.

What were Teno and Yali doing? They had gone to dig up a body buried for three millennia, topped by earth that had eroded and washed down over the years, and by oak trees two, three, five hundred years old, their roots interlaced into a barrier impenetrable as stone.

And if Dusa believed that, then she might as well believe in Gorgons and real snakes. Madness! Gently she lowered Lucy to the bed and patted her shoulder.

In the kitchen, Dusa looked at the chair. If she sat down and let herself sink deep, would the little snake come? Would it help her? She longed for help.

In her head, she heard a hissing, chuckling sound, a bit like water under a bridge. Her face prickled. Her legs were rubber, her arms lead. All of her snakes were alive and well and full of furious energy. They had never felt more powerful.

Dusa struggled back to the tower with two bottles of apple juice clutched against her body. The curving stairs mocked her. She managed them, but only just, slumping against Lucy's bed.

Lucy's eyes flew open. "What?" she whispered.

Dusa shook her head. "Not now," she gasped. She opened a bottle of juice. Lucy's high bedside table held straws. Dusa bent one and propped the bottle so Lucy could sip. Then she opened the second bottle and took several quick gulps herself. The snakes had gone, but she was, for the moment, totally drained.

Had Teno lied about the phone? Maybe it was working perfectly. More likely, one of them had disconnected something. It might be easy enough for Dusa to figure out. Maybe.

Maybe not.

"Lucy," she ventured, "if I help you, can you walk?"

"Walk?" Lucy croaked the word, then began to laugh hysterically. She burbled and wheezed, spitting pale yellow liquid onto her white sheet. In desperation, Dusa shook the thin shoulders. Lucy slumped and was silent, eyes closed.

"Lucy, say something."

"Walk?" Lucy breathed the word, her voice unutterably dreary. "What for, Dusa? Where would we walk? Off the edge of the cliff?"

"The boat," said Dusa, knowing suddenly that the cruiser had been in the back of her mind ever since Teno and Yali had brought her back to the island with the great jar on board.

Lucy stared at her. "Can you run it?" she gasped.

"Sure," said Dusa. Sure, mocked her mind. Well, she asked herself angrily, have you got a better idea?

"Help me," muttered Lucy. Dusa got an arm under the other girl's body and lifted her shoulders. How easily the thin body came up, no heavier than a big rag doll, and about as limp.

Dusa swung Lucy's legs over the side of the bed. Dubiously, she eyed the IV. It was as likely to be doing harm as good, all things considered, keeping Lucy sedated, though maybe it was feeding her as well. "Lucy," she said, "are you okay with juice?"

Lucy shrugged. "I guess."

"Let's take out the drip," said Dusa. "I can piggyback you downstairs, but not with that thing in your arm."

Lucy nodded. Her right hand reached over and picked at the tape holding the narrow tube in place.

"Let me." Dusa tugged briskly. Tape and pad pulled away. Dusa shivered.

Lucy gave the second tug. Out came the tube, followed by a gush of blood, bright scarlet against the white skin.

"Pad, in the drawer," panted Lucy, and fainted.

Dusa yanked out the drawer, scattering its contents. She tore open pads with her teeth, pressed one, two, three over Lucy's wound, held them with one hand, shook the limp body with the other. "Lucy," she hissed desperately, "Lucy, wake up, don't do this to me. Lucy!"

Once more Lucy's eyelids lifted, wearily.

"You scared me." Dusa still felt cold. Almost without

166

thinking, she tore open fresh pads, discarded the red ones, then lavishly applied adhesive tape.

It was pitifully easy to hoist the frail body onto her back. Dusa supported Lucy's bony rump with her left hand and steadied herself with her right. "Damn stairs," she muttered, curving round and round. Lucy's head was heavy on Dusa's shoulder. Lucy had tried to clasp her hands around Dusa's neck, but her grasp did not hold: she was too weak.

Bending forward, Dusa kept Lucy balanced in an awkward piggyback. She reached the bottom step at last. Now it was easier. Dusa almost ran across the office into the living room, Lucy a dead weight on her back. She rolled the limp body onto the carpeted floor and knelt, her ear pressed to Lucy's narrow chest. She could not feel any motion, could not hear a heartbeat. A sob burst from her throat.

CHAPTER 12

"What have we here?" The startled voice came from behind her. Dusa swiveled around, looking up at Yali, whose lips curled in a grimace.

"Help me." Dusa was desperate. "Help Lucy, I mean."

"How do you know her name?" Yali seemed remote, detached, interested in Dusa's answer, but not as if it was important.

"What do you mean? She told me."

"Told you!" Yali's voice changed. Quickly she knelt beside Lucy, chafing the bloodless hands. "Here, wrap her up." Rising, she tossed Dusa a handwoven throw. "Stay with her, I'll be back. Teno! Teno!" Yali's high-heeled sandals pattered off toward the lab. In a moment, Teno knelt beside the two girls, a syringe in her square hands. She rolled Lucy onto her side and lifted the cotton gown to expose her wasted buttocks.

"Hold her," she ordered.

Dusa had barely time to wonder what Teno was injecting before the needle was in, and the plunger pressed firmly home. As always in the presence of needles, Dusa felt sick and faint, but she was determined not to pass out. Yali knelt beside her. Lucy's body quivered. Quickly, Yali wrapped her again in the warm throw. Lucy sighed. Her eyes opened.

"Lucy, dear Lucy, you're back with us." She patted the body Dusa was cradling in her arms. Under the covering, Lucy shivered.

"Don't try to talk," Dusa told her. She didn't want to look at Yali or Teno. They'd likely be furious; they had a right to be.

"Yali," said Teno dryly, "we've done it again, underestimated the power of teenage curiosity. You'd think we'd know better." Dusa glanced at her.

"Have I hurt Lucy?" she burst out.

"Hurt her? It's not the way we'd have done it, Dusa, but as far as I can see, you've helped her. You've brought her out of her catatonia, which is more than we've been able to do in the past six months.

"But look here, Dusa, you'd better have more respect for the lock on the lab than you had for the one in our bedroom ceiling. I mean it. You must not even try to disturb what's happening there. If you get any wild ideas, you bring them straight to me."

"And you will get some wild ideas from Lucy," added Yali lightly, "if you haven't already." Telltale heat rose in Dusa's cheeks. "Dusa, look at me." Dusa raised her flaming face.

"So she has told you some stories already," said Yali. She laughed gently and shook her head. "Do you believe her, Dusa?"

Dusa looked down at Lucy. The faded eyes were closed. Dusa shook her head.

"It's all right, Dusa," said Teno. "We understand how confused you must be."

"Why didn't you tell me about her?" Dusa whispered.

"Put yourself in our place, if you can," said Teno. "We'd told you that you were at risk of catatonia. Stress increases the risk, Dusa. Indeed, it was the stress of some very bad news that sent Lucy over the edge. Do you think we wanted you to see her like that?"

"Especially at the start of your own treatment," added Yali. "Your stamina is developing nicely, Dusa, you've just proved it, but I'd rather not have to worry about you as well as Lucy. Have your snakes been active lately, or are you getting better since we went diving?"

"I thought I was getting better," whispered Dusa. Lucy stirred in her arms.

"You thought you were getting better, and something happened," said Teno. "It's not surprising. Are you all right now?"

"Yes," Dusa muttered.

"Good," said Teno. "Make sure you record it. We're still wearing our beepers, Dusa. Wherever we are, you can reach us if you need to. Yali, I think we will have to take turns with our archaeology. One of us had better stay with the children." There was a hint of steel in her smile.

Children! Dusa thought, feeling her face redden again.

"Can't I look after both of us?" she asked. "If we need you, we can signal. Can't you tell me what to do for Lucy?"

Lucy's eyes fluttered open. Dusa felt her trying to sit up and lifted her carefully. Teno turned over Lucy's hand and felt for her pulse.

"I'll have to examine you, Lucy," she said quietly.

"No," gasped Lucy.

"Hush," said Teno. "That's all right, child, I know your delusions. I know you are frightened of me. I understand." She looked perplexed.

"She feels the same way about me." Yali shook her head. "You will learn better in time, I hope, Lucy, but meanwhile, you believe what you believe. There's not much we can do about it. Teno, I think Lucy will have to get along without the IV. If I believed my doctors to be monsters, I would hardly allow them to put me on a drip. Am I right, Lucy?" Lucy nodded vehemently.

"The drip did its job," said Teno. "It has kept you alive in your catatonic state for the past six months. I'd rather have had you on IV for another few days while you learned to tolerate food again, but I can see that isn't going to happen.

"Thank you for offering to help, Dusa. Lucy obviously doesn't want us to take care of her. We could insist, but it would be risky when she's so weak. However, you must follow our instructions, both of you. That I do insist on. Dusa?"

"Yes, Teno."

"Lucy?"

Against Dusa's shoulder, Lucy nodded.

"Good," said Teno.

"What should I do?" Dusa asked.

"Feed her up," replied Teno. "Talk to her, though you'll do better not to believe most of what she says. Take it easy with the feeding, even when Lucy starts to get hungry. Juice, clear soup, Jell-O, hot tea with sugar would be good. Crackers. That's all for today. Tomorrow, if she feels like it, a poached egg on toast. Don't butter the toast." She glanced at Yali. "Is there anything I've forgotten?"

Yali shook her head. "Take care of each other, Dusa, Lucy. We'll get back to the lab." Teno turned toward the door, Yali following.

"Wait," called Dusa. Yali, eyebrows raised, turned back. I thought you were talking about me in the lab this morning, Dusa wanted to say, but now I think you were talking about Lucy. What are you going to do with us? she wanted to ask. When can I—when can we—go home? But as she looked at Yali, smooth as silk, impervious as stone, the questions faded.

"Nothing," said Dusa helplessly. Yali turned in a shimmer of silk and was gone.

Dusa carried Lucy into the kitchen. "I know it's hard for you to sit in a chair," she said, "but I need company. You too?"

Lucy nodded slightly. Whatever Teno had injected, it had brought Lucy out of her faint. Dusa hurried to pour more apple juice and find another straw. While Lucy sipped, Dusa mixed frozen orange juice. She heated chicken broth. She boiled the kettle and made strawberry Jell-O, putting it in the fridge to set.

172

Lucy drank a little orange juice. She drank a little warm broth.

"I'll take you into the breakfast room," said Dusa. "Soon. But I want to try something first. Don't say anything."

Quietly Dusa pulled out her chair. She sat down, put her hands on her thighs, and closed her eyes. Her breathing slowed. The little snake felt comfortable; her good companion, her ally. Dusa let herself fall.

Teno was speaking. "She's very suggestible."

"Does that trouble you?" Yali queried.

"Not seriously, but it's not ideal. Neither one of them is emotionally stable. We'll have to watch them carefully. We don't want any accidents." Teno paused, as if in thought. "Did you bring the spare boat key here, Yali?" she asked.

Dusa opened her eyes, and the contact was gone. Her eyes swung to the key rack beside the back door, where earlier she had seen a key marked "Boat." The slot was empty. Lucy, whose cheeks had shown a little pink, was now dead white again. Dusa shrugged unhappily. She gathered Lucy in her arms and carried her off to the breakfast room, plumping up cushions in the window seat behind the other girl's bony back.

Supper that evening felt very strange. On the surface, it was no different from any other evening meal on the island. Dusa had wondered if Yali and Teno would appear at all, or if they would remain in the lab. Did they really need to eat?

Promptly at six o'clock, however, Yali wheeled the loaded tea wagon into the breakfast room. Teno appeared a few minutes later, just as Dusa finished setting the table. Yali had brought a tray with soup and crackers and a second pitcher of orange juice. "How are you, Lucy?" she asked, smiling pleasantly.

Lucy shrank back into the cushions.

"Don't try to sit at the table tonight," Yali suggested. "Wait until tomorrow or the day after. You're young. You'll be surprised how fast you'll get back your strength."

"That's right," Dusa agreed. "I was weak when I got out of hospital. When we got here and we had to go up all those stairs the first time, I thought I'd never make it to the top. After a day or two, it didn't bother me."

"It won't be that fast for you, Lucy," said Teno. "Your muscles are seriously wasted. I wish Grace was here."

"Who is Grace?" asked Dusa.

"Our former physiotherapist," said Teno. "She would start Lucy on a program of massage, deep heat and very gentle exercise. I'll show you the equipment, Dusa. In a few days, you might help Lucy with some exercise. You'll have to go very slowly. Don't push, either of you."

Dusa picked up her knife and fork. Her eyes dropped to her plate. Teno was reasonable as always, yet the air felt electric with tension. Lucy had certainly made a difference. Dusa, who had felt very hungry, wondered where her appetite had gone. The entree looked like shepherd's pie, that Greek shepherd's pie, one of her favorites. She sniffed and took a bite.

"Moussaka again," said Yali. "I hope you don't mind, we've got a lot of it in the freezer."

Dusa, chewing, mumbled, "That's okay," then realized she'd been talking with her mouth full. Pearl would not be pleased.

Yali laughed. "We're celebrating tonight, Lucy," she said, raising her glass. Dark red wine glowed in the light from the iron chandelier above the table. "It's good to have you back with us. Here's to your full recovery."

Dusa clinked her glass of milk with Yali, then with Teno, and drank.

Teno nodded brusquely, and a big forkful of moussaka vanished behind her large white teeth.

"Full recovery." Was there a hidden meaning in Yali's words? Lucy's face was frozen. She made no response to the toast.

"What are you thinking, Dusa?" asked Yali.

Dusa shrugged. "Nothing much," she muttered, taking another mouthful. "You're right, I like moussaka. What's in it?"

"Ground lamb, mostly," replied Yali. "When you get back to a normal menu, Lucy, we'll have to look for bigger food packages. The three of us have been eating four portions of almost everything." She paused, then spoke brightly, in her usual psychologist's manner, "I must say, Lucy, it's a real joy to have you back. We were afraid we'd failed with you."

"Why didn't you take Lucy to a hospital in Athens?" asked Dusa curiously. "She's so thin, weren't you scared?" Scared she'd die, the words hovered, unspoken, in the air.

"We've looked after her better than anybody else could," said Teno at once. "We did everything that could possibly be done."

"Were you scared when we got here and everybody had gone?"

"Horrified," Teno rejoined. "I left Yali with you and went to Lucy at once. The nurse had hooked up a triple drip—very dangerous, it was almost empty—and abandoned her patient. Criminal negligence. She should lose her license. If you had died, Lucy, I would have gone after her, no matter what. I'm very thankful it did not come to that."

Lucy made no attempt to reply, merely stared white-faced. Had she heard anything Teno or Yali had said? Dusa's stomach was knotted, despite the excellent moussaka, but Yali and Teno seemed determined to keep the conversation going as if everything was ordinary, nothing was unusual at all. Dusa's mind skittered away again toward the pitch-lined jar that still lay on the pier, toward the snakes, toward the unknown horror in the lab.

"How are things going with you, Dusa?" Dusa jumped as Yali turned to her.

"All right," she mumbled.

"Lucy isn't ready for conversation yet. It is her first time at the table, after all. Dusa, talk to me. We did think your snakes were not giving you so much trouble. Isn't that true?"

"I haven't had any really horrible nightmares since you started the hypnosis," said Dusa quietly, "and only one seizure on the boat. That was a bad one. Wasn't it?" What was Yali after? Dusa didn't have a clue. 'We are not usually fooled,' Yali had said, and Dusa could remember being sure that they were hardly ever fooled. She had secrets now about Lucy as well as about the little snake.

"You're not so frightened of them," said Teno softly.

It was true. In the kitchen, when all her snakes had roused, Dusa had been frightened, but she did not say so. Earlier, she had chosen to welcome them; with their help, she had heard and understood Teno and Yali in the lab. The little snake was truly her friend. Dusa looked down, avoiding Teno's probing gaze.

"You did what they wanted," said Yali. "What was needed. That part of your work is done."

Dusa nodded. To her relief, Yali turned again to Lucy.

"Lucy, it's time you went to bed," she said. "Shall I carry you?"

Lucy cowered back against the pillows, shaking her head.

"No. Teno, then? No. Well, Dusa, you got her down two flights of stairs. It will be more difficult to get her up, but it seems you'll have to manage."

Lucy's white lips moved. "Not . . . back . . . there."

"All right," Yali agreed. "I'll bring a mattress and blankets here for tonight. You can sleep on the floor, Lucy, and we'll sort it out in the morning."

"Wait a minute." Dusa was shocked. "You're not sleeping alone, Lucy, and you don't have to sleep on the floor." Did she really want this crazy skeleton in bed with her? She looked at Lucy's white, closed face. "You're sleeping with me," she said.

Yali raised her eyebrows.

"It's not a bad plan," said Teno. "You're not going to lie awake whispering, I hope, not tonight. Lucy, you're still very weak." She paused, considering. "All right, I agree. Dusa, I'm sure you can get Lucy up one flight of stairs.

Give her a good wash before bed. Lucy, I'll bring your clothes. You don't need to go traipsing through our bedroom to look for her things, Dusa." She frowned. "Not that they'll fit you, Lucy, until you put on thirty pounds." She pushed back her chair.

"You look after Lucy, Dusa. I'll clean up tonight." Yali piled plates on the tea wagon. "If she faints, or if you get worried about her, call us. We'll be in the lab."

CHAPTER 13

By the time Lucy was in bed, Dusa had definitely decided not to become a nurse. Her back ached, her shoulders ached, she couldn't remember when she'd been so tired. She was proud of her results, however.

In a light blue long-sleeved sleepshirt, Lucy looked very much better. Her pale hair floated around her thin face. She badly needed a shampoo, which Dusa had refused even to consider, but with the tight braids undone and the faded hair thoroughly brushed, Lucy's face looked considerably less skeletal. She had drunk more orange juice. Perhaps because of this, there was a tiny bit of color in her cheeks.

"Thanks, Dusa," she whispered.

Dusa felt a strong urge to kiss Lucy good night like Pearl would, but compromised with a quick hug. Lucy rolled onto her side with her back to Dusa and tucked up her knees.

Dusa had expected to be asleep by the time her head hit the pillow, but she lay awake. Lucy was another snake dreamer, the first that Dusa had met. The more she thought about Lucy, however, the more questions jumped into her head. Where had Lucy come from? How long had she been on the island? Why had she made the tape asking for help? What did she know about Yali and Teno? On the tape, she talked as if she had seen them, close up, as monsters, bronze-gold scaly age-old monsters with gigantic wings and women's breasts. Had she really?

Did Lucy's parents know she had been in some kind of coma for six months? (If Dusa believed Yali, who said so, if she believed Lucy's thinness.) Why weren't Lucy's mother and father here?

What could Perse tell her about Lucy? What more could he tell her—if he was willing—about everything?

Dusa fell asleep at last.

In the morning, Lucy walked to the bathroom by herself and sat on a stool to wash her face and brush her teeth. If she was shocked to see herself in the mirror, she did not say so. "I'm starving," she announced. Her voice was husky, with a bit of an accent: sexy, thought Dusa, for the first time envious of this wraith of a girl. Dusa poured orange juice from last night's jug and carried the glass to the bathroom. Lucy made a face at the tepid drink, but gulped it down.

"I'll get breakfast," said Dusa. "Poached egg on toast."

"Thanks." Lucy's voice had lost all energy again. Returning from the bathroom, she staggered and fell weakly onto the bed.

"You should have called me!" I must not forget how frail she really is, Dusa reminded herself.

Dusa tucked the covers around Lucy and rushed off to

the kitchen, hoping to avoid Teno and Yali. Maybe the two had left already for the oak grove. Maybe they were still in the lab. She had put on the kettle, started the eggs, and got out the bread when Yali spoke behind her.

"I'm glad to see you here," she said. "Lucy must be all right, or you wouldn't have left her. How are you two getting on?" Dusa jumped, and did not turn around. She could feel Yali's golden eyes boring into her back.

"All right," answered Dusa. "She's starving." She cut four slices of bread, not at all evenly, and dropped them into the toaster.

"You need to know a few things about Lucy," said Yali, "and this is as good a time as any. Has she told you what brought on her catatonia?"

"No." Dusa turned.

Yali, resplendent in black and gold silk, frowned and shook her head. "It's tragic. Her parents were on their way to Athens for Lucy's birthday. Lucy had been with us for two years. She was doing well, and Teno was to fly her to Athens for the party." Yali paused. The golden eyes were pools of sadness.

"They were actually in the air, about halfway, when we got the news here. Lucy's father had been piloting his own small plane, a Cessna much like ours, and he had crashed. Engine failure, we learned later, and perhaps an element of pilot error. He was a competent private pilot, but not experienced in an emergency. He was killed in the crash. Lucy's mother was still alive when Lucy and Teno reached the hospital, but she died that night. Tragic, as I told you."

"How horrible! Poor Lucy." Dusa's eyes brimmed. She dashed the tears away with the back of her hand.

Yali nodded. "Poor child, indeed," she said. "Anyone would be traumatized by such an event, let alone one in Lucy's state."

"She went into a coma?" asked Dusa. "That's what catatonic means, isn't it?"

"Not exactly, but close enough," Yali agreed. "Lucy lost touch with reality almost at once. To start with, she blamed us for her parents' death. Somehow, we had caused the engine to fail! We worked with her, and our staff worked with her. We seemed to be making some progress, helping her to deal with her grief in an appropriate way, and then she fell apart again, blaming us more than ever." Yali shook her head sadly.

"She said her snakes gave her no peace, night or day, but she refused to let any of us help her. Nightmare followed nightmare, the poor girl's screams kept everybody awake. Her seizures got worse and worse, but she would not take any medication. She blamed Teno and me for everything. Indeed, she convinced herself that all snake dreamers ever born have been made that way by our evil design. Small wonder that she retreated into catatonia, seeing nothing, hearing nothing, knowing nothing."

Dusa sighed.

"Dusa," Yali's voice was low and urgent, "I must know what Lucy dreamed, if she did dream, in all those months. She still does not trust me or Teno, that's clear, but she has accepted you as a friend. She will talk to you. If she does not, you should encourage her. Whatever fantasies she comes out with, go along with her, don't disagree, don't argue, but don't for goodness' sake be sucked into believing a word of it. For Lucy's own good, Teno and I need to know what delusions she harbors now. You must tell us, Dusa, we rely on you."

"I guess," said Dusa. "It sure makes a tattletale out of me." She exhaled slowly.

"You don't want to betray her confidence," said Yali. "Sometimes, though, Dusa, telling somebody else is the only right thing to do."

"Okay," said Dusa carefully. How she loathed that phrase, "for your own good." "For Lucy's own good," she had discovered, was just as disgusting. All the same, Lucy had said some crazy things. Oh, if only she could talk to Pearl!

Dusa turned angrily back to her breakfast. The eggs would be rubbery and the toast burned.

"Here," said Yali cheerfully, as if nothing important had been said at all, "If you want to start over with the eggs, I'll do the toast. If we leave you and Lucy on your own today, can you manage?"

"Sure. What else can Lucy have to eat?"

"Small, frequent meals. Don't let her rush it, even if she says she's starving, an egg now, another one in a couple of hours, chicken and rice soup for lunch. No, avgolemono soup, it's easy, I'll show you. More juice. More broth. More Jell-O. Fish for dinner, if everything else goes well."

Yali studied Dusa for a moment. "We'll be back and forth," she said, "here and there, around and about. I'll fix dinner. Take it easy, both of you. If you need help, call us, or press the buzzer in your room. We'll carry our beepers." Off she went, slim back straight, high heels tapping, nothing monstrous about her at all. Dusa picked up the breakfast tray.

Lucy's egg and toast had disappeared before Dusa had taken more than a couple of mouthfuls. "More," she begged.

"In a couple of hours," laughed Dusa. In the daylight, her doubts seemed fantastic, her questions intrusive. She should wait until Lucy was ready to talk. If there was time. "Lucy," she began, then stopped.

"Yes?"

"Lucky you made that tape, or I'd never have known about you."

"You bet." The husky voice was fervent.

"How did you know, Lucy? How did you know about Teno and Yali?"

Lucy shivered. Her face turned white again and blank, as if she was looking inward at some vision too terrible to relate. "Sorry," said Dusa. "Think about something else. Lucy, where did you live before you came here?" She bit her tongue. She had almost come out with, "Tell me about your folks."

Lucy still had that inward look. "I see auras sometimes," she whispered, "I feel energy, in people and sometimes in objects too. It's hard to tell you, Dusa. It sounds weird, doesn't it." Dusa nodded. It sounded more than weird.

"I see shapes within shapes, shapes beyond shapes," Lucy muttered. She looked up suddenly, meeting Dusa's eyes. "I kept looking at two women and seeing monsters at the same time. Sometimes the monster looked solid and the woman looked shadowy, transparent, and sometimes the other way around. Other times, one was about as solid as the other. Almost always, I could see both shapes at the same time. Think of two naked breasts, sagging old woman's breasts, jutting out from Teno's navy jacket!" She shuddered. "I saw it before the accident. Accident, huh, it was no accident. Afterwards, it was worse. Catatonia, they called what happened to me, but I tell you, Dusa, I couldn't stand what I was seeing. I knew what they were. You can't see it, can you?" Her voice trailed off again.

Dusa muttered an uneasy, "No," then queried, "What do you see when you look at them now, Lucy?"

"I'm not seeing anything weird now, I didn't last night, but they feel weird, Dusa, Teno and Yali feel weird. You can feel that, can't you? I hate to be near them, the murderers, even if I wasn't remembering what I saw before."

"Sometimes I think they're weird too," said Dusa. But at once contrary visions rose in her head: Teno, letting her drive the boat, teaching her how to use the compass; and Yali, kind and matter-of-fact, telling her how to look after Lucy, teaching her to make soup. Were the Gordon sisters any more weird than Lucy, who saw auras? Dusa wouldn't even have known what she meant, except for a project she'd done on the occult.

Some people said they could see color radiating from a person, a band of light extending the physical form, showing the person's feelings. Red for anger, Dusa remembered. But the writer who had described auras had certainly not believed in them. She went on and on about adolescent girls and mass hysteria. As far as she was concerned, no witch would have been hanged in eighteenth-century Salem if the girls hadn't gone off the rails. To her, Lucy would be another dangerous hysterical teenage female, best locked up where she couldn't do any damage.

But so would I be, Dusa reminded herself. That author

would not believe in snake dreamers, even ones who did not see two bodies in the same space at the same time.

"Dusa," asked Lucy, "where are all the others? Have they gone?"

"Yes," said Dusa, "before I got here."

"Diana too?"

"Yes. Teno said she had run away to start her own clinic and taken all the others with her."

Lucy closed her eyes. Dusa thought she had gone to sleep, until she saw the tears. At once she knelt beside Lucy, hugging the skinny shoulders. "It's all right, Lucy, everything's all right," she muttered, chanting the words "all right" again and again, as if repetition would make them true.

The day passed slowly. Dusa made food and brought it back quickly, without sitting in the kitchen chair. Lucy ate and drowsed. In the afternoon, Dusa shampooed Lucy's fine hair, and then her own dark curls, and played at styling Lucy's hair and then her own. She put her tapes on the player. Lucy had never heard of Barenaked Ladies or the Tragically Hip. She didn't know any of the groups that Dusa liked.

"When was the last time you were in a record store?" Dusa asked, laughing.

Lucy shook her head. "Years ago," she said. "Dusa, we've got to get out of here."

Dusa looked at the buzzer on her side of the bed. If she pressed it, Teno and Yali would hear the signal. If she had a seizure, they would hear, even if she did not summon them. This room was wired. Maybe all the rooms were wired. Dusa turned up the volume and bent toward Lucy's ear.

"Can you really fly a plane?" she asked. Dusa wanted to know all about Lucy, although she had no intention of betraying her to Yali and Teno. Already, it seemed, she had made her choice of loyalties.

"I used to fly," said Lucy softly. "We had a plane in the outback."

"The outback," Dusa blurted, then whispered again. "You come from Australia! I always wanted to go there." Why hadn't she recognized the accent? It wasn't really surprising, though. Dusa didn't know any Australian girls; Lucy's accent was not strong, and much of her talk so far had been in whispers. "Sorry, Lucy," Dusa apologized quietly. "I didn't mean to interrupt. Go on."

Lucy nodded. "Dad started taking me up before I could walk. He taught me, and so did the foreman. I grew up in a Cessna. Before the snake fits got me, I was good enough to get my license, but I wasn't old enough. I never flew a float plane, but I watched Teno. I guess I could do it if I had to."

She held up her hands, so thin the sunlight seemed to shine right through them. In a moment, they began to shake. The narrow shoulders drooped. "I haven't flown a plane for years," she muttered.

"You've got to get stronger," said Dusa. "Then we can get out of here, if they haven't sent us home by then. If you can't fly, there's always the boat."

"I don't think we can wait," Lucy whispered. She sipped her orange juice. She beckoned Dusa close again and breathed softly into her ear, "They're putting Medusa together, aren't they. You helped them find her head, and now they're digging up her body. Why do I know what they're doing, and you can't see it?" Her voice turned angry, accusing.

Dusa shook her head helplessly. She liked Lucy and felt sorry for her. However, liking had nothing to do with conviction; nor did pity. One minute Dusa believed Lucy—indeed, she had reached the same conclusion; the next, she rejected that conclusion just as strongly. She had been on a dive. She had helped to raise a heavy container of some kind, pitch-lined, still smelling faintly of decay, but she had seen nothing. She had heard strange talk in a strange language, but only in fantasy, in a snake dream.

Lucy stood up, staring down at Dusa. "What's going to happen when they put Medusa back together?" she asked. "Won't they want to know if she can still do what she used to?"

Dusa put a warning finger to her lips. "I'll have to see for myself," she said.

Lucy sat down abruptly. "Good luck," she whispered bitterly. "I hope you don't get stoned when you go into the lab."

"Not the lab," whispered Dusa, grimacing at Lucy's awful pun. "The oak grove. I want to see what they're digging up. I want to look for Perse too."

"Perse!" Lucy's low voice was full of scorn. "You know where he got his name."

Dusa shook her head.

"For heaven's sake, Dusa, it's too much. Perseus killed Medusa. That was then. Now we've got Dusa and Perse."

"Oh no," said Dusa, shivering. "Whatever you're selling, Lucy, I'm not buying any. If you can look after yourself for a bit, I need to get out of here."

Dusa wanted to leave at once, but by the time she'd mixed more juice for Lucy and changed into heavy clothes and hiking boots, the sun was low in the sky. She had hardly got outside the door when she met Teno and Yali trudging along the terraced path. "I was coming to help," she blurted.

"Thanks," said Yali dryly.

"Lucy's making progress, I take it," said Teno. "That's good news. I'm glad we came back, though. Lucy is your job, Dusa. You should not leave her. We'll review the situation tomorrow, but I don't expect it to change."

Lucy joined the others at the dinner table, sitting with her back to the sea. She ate a large red snapper fillet and asked for more. She had ice cream with her Jell-O for dessert.

"Lucy, you amaze me," said Yali admiringly. "How fast you are recovering. You'll have your energy back before you know it."

"The resilience of youth," said Teno grumpily. "And no," she answered Dusa's unspoken question, "I wouldn't choose to be young again even if I could."

Soon the two sisters went off to the lab, leaving Dusa to clean up. Lucy followed her to the kitchen. "What did you do when you were in that chair?" she asked. "You could hear something, couldn't you?"

Dusa nodded slowly. "It's pretty crazy," she said. "I don't want to talk about it."

"If that's how you feel." Lucy was offhand. If her feelings were hurt, she wasn't letting on. "Do it again, if you want," she said, "whatever it is. I won't tell."

Dusa looked at her sharply. She sat down. In the kitchen chair, she felt close to the little snake, perhaps because she had welcomed him there. She closed her eyes.

In the strange language, Teno and Yali sounded different. Their voices mingled in a croon, a plaintive lament, tender, musical and sad. Tears stung Dusa's eyes; she blinked them back.

☒☒☒☒☒☒☒ CHAPTER 14

Dusa woke early next morning. On the other side of the big bed, Lucy lay, curled up and quiet, except for little pops of sound where her light breath disturbed the air.

Dusa jumped up. She sloshed water on her face, scrubbed at her teeth, waved the brush at her tangled hair. Bra and underpants, socks, olive jeans and drab turtleneck followed each other onto her wiry body.

Lucy rolled over and sat up. "You're going to the oak grove." It was not a question.

Dusa nodded. "I'll bring you something quick for breakfast." She felt driven by a sense of urgency she could not at all explain. The kitchen was empty. Plates and cups were stacked neatly beside the sink. The coffee was still hot. At the door of the lab Dusa called, "Yali, Teno," but she expected no reply and was not surprised when none came. Fresh figs and dates and a lone banana, goat cheese and dark rolls, she grabbed food from cupboards and fridge, concerned only to throw something together as fast as possible. She found the rest of the Jell-O and added it to her tray.

She whirled back to leave the tray with Lucy, munching on a fig and spitting the hard stem into her hand. She cut cheese for herself, Kasseri, hard and salty, and piled it onto thick slices of rye bread, biting into her untidy sandwich as she started down the path. The sun shone brightly, though the air was cold. The moment her hands were free, Dusa put them in her pockets, longing for a pair of leather gloves. Her way was easy at the start, but she would have to climb across the cliff face with bare hands.

When the climb was over and she faced the grove, Dusa's hands were numb. She warmed them under her arms before starting into the woods. At first she couldn't find the clearing and the stone. However much she tried to slip quietly through the trees, she kept tripping over unexpected rocks and interwoven roots. An elephant could scarcely have been noisier. She could not hope to surprise Teno and Yali. Maybe she did not want to surprise them. Maybe she wanted them to be people, neither more nor less, and not such unusual people at that.

After a few minutes Dusa heard thuds, as of earth falling, and clanging noises, as of metal on stone, accompanied by a low, plaintive song. They were making enough noise, even an elephant might not have been noticed. Dusa dropped to her hands and knees and crept closer, shivering as dampness seeped through her clothes. If only she had the cap of invisibility, she thought suddenly, the cap Perseus had borrowed in the old story, she could be on her feet, not on hands and knees.

If she could creep close enough, what would she see? A

couple of amateur archaeologists with picks and spades, or two winged monsters? A vision of two giant chickens, one with a shovel under her wing, the other with a spade, gave Dusa a mad desire to giggle. She clamped her lips shut with her teeth and crept closer.

Yali wielded the pickax. Dusa glimpsed her golden hair and saw the ax flash as she brought it heavily down. The figure was definitely Yali, dressed probably in the jeans she had worn on the boat. At first Dusa could not see Teno at all, because she was looking too high up. A flash of red drew her eyes downward, and there was Teno, her head and shoulders almost at ground level. She must be standing in a deep hole. Beyond her, the great stone still stood, but at a crazy angle.

The haunting melody stopped abruptly. Teno said something, but Dusa could not hear her voice clearly or understand her words. Yali made some reply, then stooped with something—ropes? netting?—trailing from her hands.

Dusa inched forward. A small branch snapped under her, and she froze again, bending her dark head to the ground. She couldn't see anything clearly, and couldn't understand anything she heard. On TV shows, the watcher always managed to sneak up almost beside the scene of action, and the actors conveniently spoke English and enunciated each word with clarity.

In real life, Dusa decided, spying, like nursing, was a career to avoid. She lifted her head. Yali and Teno had rigged another block and tackle, on the same principle as they had used on the boat. Dusa could see the pulleys clearly; the rope had been thrown over a huge branch of one of the vast oak trees, at least twenty feet from the ground, and her angle of vision was uninterrupted.

What were they about to lift from that hole?

"Are you ready?" asked Teno, from below.

"Not quite," came Yali's calm reply. "This is a great moment in our lives, Teno, and in our favorite hobby. Let's not rush it."

Dusa breathed more easily. Whether the two sisters had switched from Greek to English, or whether they had been speaking English all along and Dusa's ears had suddenly become attuned to their speech at this distance, she could now hear every word as clearly as if this were a television performance after all.

"How many archaeologists have had such an opportunity?" Yali went on. "When we publish, Teno, I believe our reputations will rival those of Carnarvon or Schliemann."

"We are not looking at another Tutankhamen," said Teno, "nor the ruins of another Troy. No, this is far more wonderful." Her voice vibrated with passion.

Dusa shivered.

"Ready away," said Teno at last. "Hoist!" Yali seized the rope and began to back away from the hole, pulling as she went. The rope creaked through the set of pulleys. Above the hole, Dusa could see an enormous hook. Something— ropes, a net perhaps—was suspended from the hook.

Yali kept backing up. In horror, Dusa suddenly realized that Yali was moving on an angle that would bring her, if she kept going, much too close. She wouldn't trip over Dusa, but she could hardly miss seeing her. Now Dusa wanted to get away worse than she had previously wanted to get near.

Yali paused, still without looking in Dusa's direction, and tied her rope around a tree. "I'm coming back," she called to Teno, "just for a minute. How's it coming?"

"Perfectly," Teno called back, "but yes, Yali, come and see for yourself."

Yali tramped noisily back to the hole, and Dusa slipped and slithered her way back out of the grove and crept across the rock face, where her feet were growing accustomed to the tiny ridges, and her hands did not have time to grow numb.

Back in the tower room, the Barenaked Ladies tape was already loud. Lucy sat motionless on the window cushions as Dusa described her expedition.

"They heard you," she whispered, with a look of disgust. "Dusa, it was a setup. Don't you see? All that stuff that made you think of TV, they were putting on a show, all right, and that show was all for you. You fell for it."

"I don't think so," Dusa answered doubtfully. It did make a certain horrid sense.

"You were conned," said Lucy. "They looked normal, they dug normal, they talked normal, normal *English*. Come on, Dusa. Do you really think that proves they *are* normal? You're smarter than that."

"I guess so," said Dusa, then wondered if she was agreeing because she was supposed not to argue with Lucy, or because she strongly suspected that Lucy had got it right. "You've seen them as monsters," she tried to explain. "I want to see something too, but I can't."

"It's hard for you," Lucy sympathized. She shrugged. "You must be starving. Let's go for lunch."

They went down to the kitchen, and Dusa opened the fridge, then closed it abruptly. A muffled, clanking noise drew her to the back door, Lucy at her heels. The noise continued, but they could not see anything.

"I'm going out," said Dusa softly. "Close the door after me."

The wide, garage-style outer door of the lab was set into the same wall as the kitchen door where Dusa now stood. If Yali and Teno were bringing something from the oak grove, the lab was almost certainly their destination. From where she stood, Dusa had an excellent view of the big door; unfortunately, anyone approaching that door would have an excellent view of Dusa. The nearest shelter was the little garden shed. Dusa ran and slipped inside. She waited. Five minutes went by, then fifteen, then half an hour. The clanking noise continued. What could it be?

Dusa was about to look for a better vantage point when the procession came in sight. Yali and Teno were dragging a stone box. It was about the size of a small car—or, thought Dusa, a large coffin. A heavy chain went around it like a string around a parcel; the stone box and the chain thumped and clanged across the rocky ground. Yali and Teno gasped with effort. They wore harnesses of wide canvas; even so, the task must have been prodigious. Could any two humans drag such a weight?

Step by step, Teno and Yali trudged toward the lab, stopping some twenty feet away. Both dropped their harnesses. Teno stepped up briskly and worked the combination, slipping under the big door as it rose. She emerged a moment later, dragging the end of another chain, which she hooked onto the box. Yali vanished into the lab. A motor whirred, the chain drew taut, and the coffin shape jerked forward, then moved steadily across the last few feet of ground and screeched, metal and stone on concrete, as it entered the building. The door closed with a small thud.

"They'll be in the lab for hours, likely," Dusa reported.

Lucy nodded grimly. "Let's have lunch," she said, "then we can decide what to do next."

Dusa cooked lamb sausage in the microwave and tried to pretend it was hot dogs. Cheese dogs, with goat cheese. She felt homesick for ordinary hot dogs and plain white hot dog rolls, even for Kraft slices, which she had despised for years. She slathered her sausage with mustard. She and Lucy munched, and Dusa's spirits began to rise. She was eating Yali and Teno's food. Why should it not enable her to perceive their real selves, whatever those might be? When Lucy gestured toward the chair, Dusa nodded.

At first she heard nothing except little squeaks and rustles, little thumps. At last, Teno's voice, flat, toneless, "Nothing."

Yali's voice, "Let's try it this way." More little thumps. "No, it's no good."

"She looks splendid, doesn't she. There must be some way, we just haven't found it yet."

Dusa shivered. The tone of the voices in the lab, more than their actual words, spooked her. She opened her eyes. "Do you think you can fly the plane?" she whispered.

"Look at me." Lucy held out translucent, unsteady hands.

"Sorry I asked. We'll have to use the boat."

"You agree we have to get away. I'm glad," said Lucy softly. "We must have a key for the boat."

"Impossible," muttered Dusa. "The spare key is in the lab."

"Where in the lab? Do you know?"

Dusa remembered hooks to the left of the door. There, maybe. "We'll get in," Lucy whispered. "When we do, close your eyes and feel your way. Whoever gets the keys should take them all, then call out, and we'll both turn around and get out of there. Don't you dare open your eyes until you've got your back to that room. Then run for the boat. Whatever happens, don't look back." The soft voice in Dusa's ear sounded strong and confident, so much that Dusa had a fantasy of the plane in the air, with Lucy at the controls.

The kitchen door flew open. Yali stood in the entrance, once more clean and shimmering, despite her work with the pickax. Teno was right behind. Around them, menace darkened the air.

Dusa shuddered, gazing at Yali. Golden eyes locked with sapphire. Yali broke the silence. "Remember, I said I'd tell you when we found something interesting. We said we'd let you see what we're doing."

"I remember," said Dusa. "When you were sure it's safe."

Yali didn't miss a beat. "Exactly," she replied. "Come along, both of you."

Dusa turned to look at Lucy. In her head, the snakes clamored and would not be stilled. Lucy stood up, squaring her thin shoulders. How frail she looked.

Dusa turned back to Yali. "I think we should wait until later," she said. "My snakes seem to be telling me that. Besides, we haven't finished our lunch." The remains of the lamb sausage, congealed in an ugly mixture of cheese and mustard, mocked her from the plate.

"Your snakes are excited, are they?" asked Yali. "I can tell. You're wrong about the reason. They want you to come with us."

"Right now," Teno insisted.

"They are *my* snakes." Dusa tried to sound confident. "You don't know what they want."

"*My snakes*," mimicked Teno. "Aren't you bold, all of a sudden. We'll see whose snakes they are! I thought you'd be crying for your mommy, moaning and groaning because the phone doesn't work."

Dusa blinked. What are you doing? she wanted to ask. Why, Teno, why?

"Dusa," said Lucy quietly, "don't let them get to you. We don't have to go with them."

Yali pounced. "Of course you don't," she agreed. "It was a silly idea to invite you. Teno, I told you it was a silly idea, didn't I?"

"You did," said Teno. "It would be too much for you, Lucy. But you want to come, don't you, Dusa: Miss Curiosity Thrasman. You could no more walk away from the chance to find out what we're doing than a moth could fly away from a candle flame." Teno's dark eyes glittered with fearful energy. Dusa could feel that energy sapping her will; even her snakes were subdued.

"Teno, you shouldn't provoke Dusa," said Yali at once. "It isn't called for. Lucy failed, but Dusa did not. You deserve to know everything, Dusa. After all, you made it possible, no one but you." Yali's voice sank into a hypnotic tone and rhythm.

Dusa took one step forward, then another. Of course she wanted to see what had happened. Of course she wanted to go into the lab. She had been there once, when she first arrived. She recalled a big room, white and sterile, with jars and bottles on the shelves, locked cupboards above steel sinks and counters, some empty cages that might once have held white rats. Dusa was sure she had recently been frightened of the place, but she could not imagine why.

Lucy looked at Yali, a long, considering look. Then she moved quickly in front of Dusa. "I'm going too," she announced.

Teno laughed. She turned and led the way along the corridor. Dusa followed Lucy. Yali's heels tap-tapped behind.

At the door, Lucy extended her left hand back to Dusa, who reached out to grasp the older girl's warm fingers. The sudden contact cleared her mind, and she shuddered convulsively. "Close your eyes," whispered Lucy. Dusa heard the door open and felt cool air on her face. Then without warning her nose filled with the smell of something indescribable, the stench of the thing on the pier but a thousand times intensified. In her head, the snakes went mad. Dusa pulled back in revulsion, jerking Lucy, who stumbled into her.

She felt herself pushed aside by Yali's strong, slim fingers, heard the tap-tapping of Yali's high-heeled shoes.

"The key," said Lucy. "I've got it. Here." Lucy pressed

cool metal into Dusa's palm. "Keep your eyes shut, Dusa."
Then, "Omigod!"

The hand Dusa was holding, Lucy's hand, turned suddenly cold and stiff and heavy. Dusa's other hand went out in front of her automatically, as she tried not to lose her balance, but the space where Lucy had been was empty. Right in front of her, something smashed thunderously to the floor. Dusa felt the shock waves as she herself pitched forward. Under her weight, something snapped and shattered.

Dusa knew she was supposed to be holding the boat key, but her hands were empty. She must have dropped it. On hands and knees, she scrabbled on the floor, which seemed to be covered with some sort of debris. Wherever the precious key had fallen, she would never find it without opening her eyes. Dusa's eyes, however, seemed to be glued shut. She forced herself to open them the tiniest bit. Squinting, she looked down at the floor.

The concrete was dusty. Dusa was kneeling on something hard and sharp. A gleam of metal caught her eye: the key. Her hand gathered it up, along with a chunk of something else. Now she was aware of commotion beyond her in the lab: voices raised exultantly, screams of joy, loud sounds of hissing. In her head, the snakes hissed in frenzied response.

Dusa began to look up. "No!" screamed the little snake. "Shhhhut your eyesssss!" Dusa closed them. It was not a thinking process. Dusa was not thinking. Her stomach heaved; vomit rose sharp in her throat, and she swallowed it down. Slowly she pushed herself upright, her eyes still closed, and emptied her hand into her pants pocket.

"So it begins." Yali's voice was thick with triumph.

Teno's echoed eerily, "So it begins."

Now Dusa heard a third voice, full of sorrow. "So it continues." The silence stretched and stretched.

"She was my daughter, as you are my sisters, blood of my blood, I felt it. There is yet another, here in this room. Cover your eyes, my daughter, and keep them covered and closed; for your life, keep your eyes closed."

Dusa could not reply. If she fainted and her hands fell away and her eyes opened, what then?

"Don't faint," commanded the voice, vibrating through her. "Small snake that loves her, help this child of mine."

Dusa's knees buckled. "Danger," cried the little snake in her head, and Dusa felt them there, her own snakes, giving her strength. In a sudden burst of energy she turned, ready to open her eyes and run. Behind her, she could not see Teno's upraised hand, or the heavy bottle in it, or the sudden blow that struck her down.

When Dusa woke, her hands were tied behind her. Her eyes were covered with something heavy and very thick.

"If that's what you wanted, you've brought me back for nothing," she heard. "Maybe you want to whack off my head again, and put it on another shield."

"How can you talk like this? After everything!" It was Teno's voice, barely recognizable through the overlay of rage.

"Teno," Yali sounded calmer, "we must not blame the victim. Our sister is the victim, we must not forget." Her voice altered, wheedling, "Surely, dear sister, you won't let these petty human lives get in our way. You are coming into your power, dear one, after all these centuries."

"Am I coming into my power," asked the unknown voice, "or are you coming into yours? I have not forgotten the days of long ago, Stheno, Euryale, even if you have forgotten them. You longed for power even then."

"Why would we not?" Teno said passionately. "Athene herself gave you that power, no matter that she intended it as punishment. It was not deserved, we all know that. Why not use the weapon she gave?"

"These humans don't deserve death or slavery now any more than I did then. Go away, sisters; leave me with this child. You know our bond."

"You are bonded by the snakes," said Teno slowly. "Despite all our knowledge, we could not really control them."

"Not totally," said the voice. "In the end, the snakes were always mine, and my children's, down the centuries."

"This discussion is not finished," said Yali, "but we will leave you, won't we, Teno."

"For the moment," Teno coldly agreed.

Dusa heard their footsteps, and the closing door.

"Now, little daughter, we shall talk."

The stench seemed less overpowering; Dusa's stomach no longer heaved. Perhaps I'm getting used to it, she thought, though the idea was hard to believe. Involuntarily, her nostrils wrinkled.

"I don't like it either," said the voice quietly, "though I've lived with it for so long. I would smell sweeter for you, little daughter, if I could."

"I'm sorry." Dusa felt her face turning red.

"No matter. Put it aside. We have much to tell each other, and little time. If I hand you a mirror, child, do I dare take the bandage off your eyes?"

"Did you turn Lucy to stone?" Dusa asked.

"Whatever happened, I wished her no harm." The voice was sorrowful. "She should not have seen my face. I will keep my mirror, Dusa, and your eyes will remain covered. You, above all humans, must be kept safe."

"Why me 'above all'?"

"Don't you understand? It's thanks to you that I am here, thanks to you that my head no longer lies in an urn at the bottom of the ocean, where it has lain for more centuries than I like to think of. Thanks to you, I will feel sun and rain on my face; I will spread my wings and ride the winds once more."

"And kill people, thanks to me?"

"I never wished to kill anyone. Dusa, you have read the old stories as they have come down to your time. Do those stories show me seeking out humans to destroy them?"

"No," Dusa admitted. "Perseus used your head as a murder weapon. He seemed to enjoy it. I think he was disgusting."

"I didn't like him myself," the voice was clearly amused. "Dusa, child, it was so long ago."

"Tell me."

"In me, victim and killer come together." Dusa quivered; she remembered saying those words. Medusa's voice was fierce. "First Perseus, then Athene, I was their weapon, nothing more. When the goddess had no more use for it, she put my head in a jar. Yes, Dusa, the very jar you found."

"Athene buried that jar in the ocean?"

"No! She gave it to my enemy Poseidon. The sea god buried the urn. 'No one will ever raise you, I'll make sure of that,' he said. And no one did, for thirty centuries."

"I can't get my mind around it," said Dusa honestly. "I haven't been here on the island for thirty weeks, and it seems like forever. Three thousand years! How could you stand it?"

"Anger kept me going for a long time," Medusa replied. "Rage—at Perseus, at Athene, at all the unjust gods. I raged at humans too. If they had not wanted to kill each other, they would have had no use for me."

"I guess you would have turned all of them to stone," said Dusa sadly.

"I might have, as many as I could, if I had got out then. But energy dies," Medusa went on. "After many centuries, my rage had burnt out completely. All my senses had grown dull. Sometimes I longed for sunlight, or for the dancing ocean waves, but without hope, without intensity, and less as the centuries passed. For an eon, I lay in that urn, almost dead myself."

Under the bandage, Dusa's eyes filled with tears. A sniffle escaped her.

"You're crying!" Medusa's voice quivered.

Dusa felt something soft, wiping her cheeks. "It's so awful," she sobbed, "it's so, so unfair."

"It *was* awful," said Medusa gently. "It *was* unfair." Dusa's sobs gradually subsided. "You ended it, Dusa, little daughter, you and your snakes."

"Did I really?"

"Yes, indeed. Without you, I would still have been at

the bottom of the sea." She paused. "You didn't do it all by yourself, of course."

"Yali and Teno did a lot," said Dusa hesitantly.

"They did," Medusa agreed. "They might have given up, and they did not. They did great harm, though. Many of my daughters have suffered and died because of them."

"What do you mean?"

"I'm angry at my sisters, Dusa. They must not do more harm. Are you sure you want more of this story? It's not pretty."

"You said Teno and Yali hurt us? They helped snake dreamers here at the clinic, didn't they?"

"Yes and no," Medusa said. "I've been listening to them, here in the lab, while they tried to put me together. They did not know it, but sometimes I could overhear what they were saying. It's clear enough what happened.

"Back in the urn, you remember, there wasn't much life in me. I thought my snakes were no better, but I was wrong. My littlest one is the twin of yours, Dusa; he never gives up. He roused the others, and they reached out. Here and there, they made contact with my daughters, and my daughters dreamed of snakes.

"They were not nightmares, those dreams, not at first. The dreamers did not become ill. However, Yali and Teno, searching the earth for traces of me, came upon them. Searching for me, my sisters found ways to amplify the snake dreams. They brought snake dreamers here to this island where we had lived in the old times, and captured a son of Perseus to be their slave."

"Why?"

"It was the ideal focus for all the energy they could gather, the place where my snakes would speak most loudly to their counterparts. Teno and Yali were right about that. The result, though, was to amplify snake dreams everywhere, so strongly that the dreams often destroyed the dreamers. Yali and Teno put all snake dreamers at risk."

Dusa shivered. "Didn't they cure any?"

"They cured a few of them." Medusa sighed. "My snakes were desperate, Dusa. They could not see what happened to the girls whose snakes answered their cries. They intended no harm." She resumed, briskly. "Then you appeared on the scene. You were stronger than any other snake dreamer they had met, and your snakes were more powerful. Over and over, my snakes made contact with yours. Unlike other girls, you were not destroyed by those contacts. You know what happened after that. My snakes guided yours and showed them my ocean burial place."

"I thought it was like that." Dusa smiled.

"Our snakes connect us," Medusa repeated. "We are both strong. Sometimes only a strong woman or man can resist the impulse to destroy."

Dusa shivered. "You resisted it."

"I am resisting it, and I will resist. Because of my need, Teno and Yali were able to gather energy here. My snakes used that energy to help you find me. Now the need is past. Snake dreams will not be amplified any more. There will be no more seizures, no more catatonia and death."

"I'm glad," cried Dusa. "But—I'll miss my little snake!"

Medusa laughed. "Think, Dusa! I didn't say there would be no more snakes! Your little snake will be there. He lies deep in your mind, but you know how to summon him."

"He was my friend."

"He is still your friend, and the agent of our bond. From time to time, you will surely feel my love. In need, you may call on my strength and some part of it will be yours."

"Give me the mirror," said Dusa. "Turn me away from you and untie my hands so I can get this black thing off my eyes. I have to see you. I want to remember you always."

"I warn you, child, I don't look any better than I smell. Do you really want to see?"

"We have a bond," said Dusa. "Your voice is full of love. Let me see your face."

"We must hurry, then. My sisters will not stay away much longer. You must be gone before they return."

Dusa felt rough hands on her wrists. The ties fell away. The chair she sat in was lifted, turned, and set down again. "Hold this," said Medusa's voice. Dusa felt something thrust into her hands. "Let me uncover your eyes. Don't try to do it yourself; it would be too easy to drop the mirror. I am standing behind you, on your left. Tilt the mirror.

"You will see that my face is hideous," she said calmly. "But you have always known the wonder of my snakes. Perhaps their beauty outweighs my ugliness."

In the mirror, Dusa looked at Medusa. She had steeled herself to hide horror and revulsion. Instead, she felt understanding and empathy. She saw the ocean of pain in Medusa's deep, dark eyes. The face was grotesque: huge mouth, protruding teeth, one eye higher than the other; the proportions were horrid.

In the hospital back home, before she had ever heard of the Gordon Clinic, Dusa had had a roommate for a week, the victim of a dreadful fire. The woman's bandages were taken off while she was prepared for another in a long series of operations, and Dusa had seen the scarred and twisted travesty that was usually hidden from the world. She knew her roommate's history by this time; she wept when she saw the ruined face. As she looked at Medusa's face in the mirror, her eyes filled with tears. To her amazement, Medusa's mismatched eyes also brimmed and overflowed.

The mirror trembled in Dusa's hand, reflecting the snaky halo that framed Medusa's face. Dusa's own snakes were magnificent, but they were pale imitations of these. Dusa caught her breath. Gold, sapphire, diamond, emerald, ruby and glittering jet undulated in and out of her vision in a graceful dance. Two great golden snakes twisted around each other, glowing like lambent flames. A little black snake, sapphire-striped like her own but far more brilliant, weaved and bobbed. In her head, Dusa felt an echo of its mischievous laughter.

"Enough," said Medusa at last. "As a Gorgon, I have great wings and sharp claws. Like my sisters, however, I can take on human form. I'll show you how I looked when I was human, before the old gods had their way with me."

Dusa moved. "Don't turn around, child!" screamed Medusa. "For your life, don't turn. Stone cannot revert to human flesh." She drew a deep breath. "Don't drop the mirror, Dusa. I know I frightened you. Let us sit quietly until you stop trembling. If you are able, my far-off little daughter, I would like to hold your hand."

They sat together, one behind the other, holding hands. Medusa's hand felt sinewy and very strong.

Dusa stared intently, moving the mirror to show this part and that of the form behind her. As far as she could see, Medusa was not stocky like Teno, but she appeared more muscular than Yali and darker-skinned. Except in one detail, Medusa's human head provided a complete contrast to the Gorgon one. Her face was olive-colored, oval, and well proportioned, with a large and generous mouth. However, her glorious snakes also cascaded around Medusa's human countenance.

"You could have shown me this form and not the other one," Dusa said at last.

"Yes. Are you glad or sorry that I showed you both?"

"Glad. I want to know all about you. I'm glad you kept your snakes, though. What color was your hair, before you had snakes?"

"I can't remember." Medusa chuckled. "Black, I think."

"Snakes are more interesting," said Dusa thoughtfully. "I love your snakes."

Medusa's dark eyes twinkled.

"Gorgon or human, which will you remember?"

"Both, of course. They are both you, aren't they?" Dusa sat dreamily absorbing the warm comfort of Medusa's loving hand, clasped tightly around her own.

Medusa drew a deep breath. "Go now," she said. "I tell you again, we can touch each other sometimes in our minds. You can summon me through your snakes. Wherever I am, be certain, I will come."

210

"I don't want to leave you."

"You must. We should not have waited so long. Teno and Yali are hungry for power, Dusa. They intend to use you to control me; they will be desperate to keep you here. I will delay them. When they fly after you, I will fly as well. I'll distract them. I'll get in their way. Whatever you do, Dusa, when you hear us, don't look up. Take this mirror with you, don't waste time looking for one on the boat. Go, child, go."

The strong hand pushed. Dusa, mirror in hand, stumbled toward the door. She never remembered her last descent of the zigzag stairs, nor did she remember collapsing on the pier. Some time later, she came to, shivering with cold. Hands slapped at her, none too gently. Water, cold as ice, stung her face. She licked her lips and tasted salt. She recalled once more the sudden hardness, coldness, heaviness of Lucy's final grasp and the fearful danger of Medusa's face. Her eyes opened. She shut them instantly in terror, but then realized she had glimpsed brown hands, brown eyes, and chestnut curls.

Perse!

Dusa opened her eyes again. Perse sighed. "The gods be thanked," he muttered.

"Where's your jacket?" It felt like a silly question even as she asked, but Perse's arms were bare. She caught his glance and felt the coarse wool around her, between her and the frozen ground. She struggled to sit up. Perse's arm came around her shoulders.

On one side of the pier, the Cessna rocked and tugged at her moorings; on the other, the *Euryale* did the same, her outsize fenders bumping against the wooden pilings.

The day was bright, but the raw wind tore at the two young people cruelly, and dark storm clouds were gathering in the west.

Automatically, Dusa looked up, but there was no sign of pursuit. She clutched the mirror. "Perse, we've got to get out of here," she said, shakily. "They'll be after us any second." She felt her pocket. "I've got the key for the *Euryale*."

Perse nodded. He picked Dusa up, held her against him. His arms were cold. Still carrying her, he stepped aboard the boat and felt for the catch on the cabin door. It was cold inside too, but felt warmer out of the wind.

"Key," said Perse. Dusa gave it to him.

Perse studied the controls. He pushed a chrome lever, pressed and held a button, and turned the key. The engines roared.

"You're coming with me," said Dusa thankfully.

Perse shrugged. "Can't go, can't stay," he said unhappily. "I help you, Dusa. Here, look." He guided her hand at the controls. "After two minutes, do this. Then boat can go. Do this, boat go fast fast. Do this, slow slow."

"Teno showed me," said Dusa, remembering. "But you'll be here if I forget."

Perse smiled, a strangely beautiful smile, another memory that would be imprinted on Dusa's mind.

"Compass here," he pointed. "I not knowing what way is best. North something, maybe. You go same way, keep going, no change, you get someplace for sure."

Dusa's jaw dropped. "No, Perse, come with me, you've got to come." She clutched at him. He put his arms around her. They held each other. Dusa rested her head against his shoulder. She could feel the throb of his pulse.

They heard a screech and looked up. Two great bronze shapes launched themselves from the terrace, spreading vast wings to catch the wind.

"Don't look," cried Dusa.

"I cast off," said Perse, loosing himself from Dusa's arms. "I cast off, you go. I be okay here. I hope." He leaned forward. His lips touched hers lightly, like a feather, and he was gone.

Dusa eased the throttle; the roar of the diesels slowed to a purr. In the quiet, ropes thudded against the *Euryale*; the big fenders thumped as they were thrown onto the deck.

"Go!" screamed Perse.

D usa glimpsed two bronze shapes hurtling toward her. She felt their rage. Blindly she engaged the gears and pushed the *Euryale* to her top speed. The cruiser surged forward, her wake spraying out astern. Waves of her making crashed against the pier. After a minute, Dusa tilted the mirror and looked back toward the island. Against the cliff, she saw the gleam of bronze. She pushed at the throttle again, but it did not move; the *Euryale* was already doing her best. When Dusa looked again, the miniature castle still showed white against the blue sky, a tower at each end, and she could faintly see the steps zigzagging their way down the cliff, but that was all.

She set her course due north and did not budge for the next hour. When she could wait no longer, she throttled back to neutral and went forward to the head. Around her, sky and sea had turned gray. The island had disappeared. Unless the clouds blew away, there would be no sunset and no stars.

Where were the charts? She made a cursory search, but

abandoned it after a few minutes. How could a chart help her? Dusa had no idea where the island was located. The flight from Athens had taken—what?—a couple of hours, but Athens could be anywhere. Had they flown mostly over land or sea? Cloud cover had hidden the ground much of the time.

Perse was right, one course was pretty much as good as another. She had to be somewhere in the Mediterranean. Africa must be south of her, and Europe more or less north. All she had to do was stay on course, and she must sooner or later reach land. If the fuel lasted. If there was nothing wrong with the compass. If no sudden storm came up. If she didn't crash on an unseen shoal. She motored on, alone in the gray world.

The cruiser was fitted with an autohelm, but Dusa did not know how to set it up, let alone how to use it. She tried several possibilities, without success. As the hours wore on, her shoulders and neck ached more and more. Twice she left the wheel to use the head, and once to look for food. She took bread and cheese and a soft drink back to her perch. Two or three times she drowsed off and roused again, slapping her face and pinching her hands.

At last Dusa knew she could not keep herself awake any longer. She wondered if she should try to drop anchor, but in the darkness the idea was too much to contemplate, and even if she got the winch turned on and the anchor down, she wasn't sure she could get it up again. A minute later she recognized the folly of even attempting to anchor: she did not know the depth of the sea below her, nor did she know the length of the anchor chain.

The sea was fairly calm. Nervously, Dusa pushed the

stop button, and the sound of the engines died. She went down to her berth, but tonight it felt claustrophobic and dangerous rather than cozy, and she took comforters and pillows back to the main cabin near the wheel, falling asleep almost at once on the carpeted floor.

Dusa woke to another gray day. She was curled in a comforter, snug and cozy, and would not have moved, except that something sharp jabbed at her hip. She felt underneath her and turned so that she could put her hand in her pocket and remove the object, which turned out to be a piece of quartz, shaped rather like a stubby pencil, perhaps three inches long.

Then Dusa remembered Lucy's hand growing cold and hard in her grasp. The stench of the lab rose again in her nostrils. The crash of stone shattering on a concrete floor rang in her ears. She held the object closer, turning it over with icy hands. Her stomach contracted. Just in time, she lurched through the door and vomited over the rail.

For a while Dusa thought she would faint and tumble into the waves, and this would not be a bad ending; but it did not happen. It was a long time, however, before she stopped retching. She had dropped the stony shape and could not find it again, but the picture was etched in her mind: the hangnail she had promised to clip for Lucy as soon as she found her clippers had formed a tiny protrusion in the pink-white stone, against the indentation that had once been a human fingernail.

Wind and rising waves roused her some hours later. She started up again and chugged on lethargically, more or less northward, but her attention wandered often from the compass. The engines stopped in midafternoon. Dusa had not looked at the fuel gauge for hours; she was not surprised to find it showing empty. A red alarm flashed and little beeps sounded. She would no doubt have seen the signal or heard it, if she had not been so deep in exhausted wretchedness. What difference would it have made? None at all. The cruiser pitched and wallowed.

An idea came to her, a vague memory that a flag flown upside down was a signal of distress. Dusa stared at the blue-and-white flag flying from a short pole at the *Euryale*'s stern. She leaned over, one hand clenched on the rail. The flag was tied, top and bottom, to brass clips. The rope was wet, the knots almost impossible to loosen with her one free hand.

Once she had begun, however, Dusa hated to give up, though it seemed unlikely that her signal would ever be seen. Shivering in the biting wind, she dug in the locker for rope which she tied around her waist and then, as tight as she could manage, around the rail. She would cut the flag loose if she had to. With two hands available, however, her trembling fingers freed it and she caught the bright cloth, turning it so that the white cross (Saint George's cross, Yali had told her, Saint George who killed the dragon) was at the bottom, not the top. Dusa's knots were clumsy. The upside-down flag was not tidy; she could only hope it was secure.

Dusa dragged her pillow and comforters back to the little berth, climbed into bed and closed her eyes. She thought of that distant foremother who cared about her and had tried to save her. She thought of Pearl, who would never know what had happened. It seemed a pity, but not something she could do anything about, and not hugely important.

A shout wakened Dusa from a nightmare in which three bronze creatures soared, screaming, above the boat. She was stiff and very cold, her bedding clammy and wet. Her throat ached. Above her, dark faces peered and babbled. She tried to sit up and fell back again. She was vaguely aware of being lifted in a man's arms, of a scratchy sweater stinking of fish and sweat, of a cup being held to her mouth. She gagged, then swallowed. Coffee, sweet and hot. She closed her eyes again.

At the Canadian Embassy in Athens, the duty man that Sunday afternoon cursed his luck. The morning had been quiet. He had drafted one complicated letter, then had caught up with the Toronto, Montreal and Vancouver papers. He had brought his warm track suit and down-filled parka to the office, intending to close early and take his beloved Wayfarer out for an hour or two before dinner. Many sailboats had been pulled out for the winter; his would follow them soon. He could almost feel the cold wind on his cheeks; he could almost smell the sea.

The vision evaporated as his secretary burst into the office with the news that three Greek men had dumped a girl and a Canadian passport in the reception room and left again. "They said they had been fishing, and I believe it," she added, wrinkling her nose. "They said they had to go and look after their fish. It's a weird story, what there is of it. They found a cruiser drifting not far off the shoals, out of gas, no one at the helm. Nobody was aboard except this girl. To hear them tell it, they saved her life. She had this passport in her bag. That's all they know, they told me, but they said they would phone us tomorrow. Maybe they will, maybe not. To tell you the truth, I thought they were scared. The girl is in a bad way, sir, I expect we'll have to take care of her."

"Damn," said the duty man, and came. He studied the Canadian passport and decided that the emaciated and feverish young woman might once have been the vivacious teenager in the photo. He could make no sense of her muttering, but clearly she needed medical attention. He summoned an ambulance and rode with it, arranging for Dusa's admittance to hospital and for her treatment there.

"Thrasman," it was not a common name. Where had he heard it recently? He jostled his memory. Wasn't that the name of the woman who had wanted information about a psychologist? Then she had wanted to hire a plane to take her to an island, only she didn't know where the island was. She was looking for her daughter, wasn't she? Maybe they shouldn't have laughed so hard. Diplomatic training has its uses, he mused, thankful that they had not laughed until the door had closed behind her. He looked for the file, and telephoned the woman's hotel.

Thanks to him, Pearl was dozing in a chair by Dusa's bed when her daughter began to stir.

"Mom?" Dusa's hoarse whisper woke her mother instantly. She held Dusa and rocked her; they cried in each other's arms. An IV tugged painfully at Dusa's hand. "What's this for?" she asked thickly, but did not wait for an answer. "Mom, thank goodness you're here."

They hugged each other again and again, but did not talk much that day, or the next, though Dusa looked much better. "How come you were here when I woke up?" Dusa asked.

"I've been here for two weeks," Pearl replied. "I was frantic, not talking to you, not knowing if you were all right, so I came. Much good did it do me! As far as I can find out, nobody in Athens has ever flown to that island except Yali and Teno. Some people know about the clinic, but nobody knows how to get there." I can't tell her about Diana's phone call, not when she's so weak, Pearl said to herself. I can't tell her that when I got here, Diana was gone.

Dusa wanted to tell Pearl about Medusa, and about Lucy, and all the rest of it, but she couldn't find a place to begin. Just thinking about it made her tired. What would she do if Pearl didn't believe her?

The fishermen did come back to the embassy to ask after the girl they had rescued. "With her luck, that girl should buy lottery tickets, she'd win for sure," they said. "Half an hour later, fifteen minutes maybe, we'd have missed her in the dark. We wouldn't even have been there, wherever it was, if our engine hadn't quit. It's a good engine, never gives us trouble, except that day.

"Who knows how long she was drifting? Why was she by herself in that big boat? Crazy kid! No fuel, and she wasn't far from the shoals, she'd never have lasted the night. She cried a lot. Sometimes she screamed. Out of her head, you understand. She's better now? That's good.

"The boat?" The speaker shivered. "We don't want no salvage rights out of her. *Euryale*, not a lucky name, not a lucky boat. We don't want no part of that boat."

The man from the Embassy visited the hospital, delighted to see Dusa looking so much more like the pretty curly-head in her passport photo. Soon she and her mother would be going back to Canada. First, however, he must have information from her so that he could complete his report. Where were the owners of the cruiser? How could he contact them? Did she have their permission to drive the boat? How did she come to be in it all alone? He wondered if he should talk to the police.

Dusa tried to explain about the island, to tell why she needed to leave so suddenly, but stopped abruptly as she saw his kindly face becoming blank and guarded. She knew that look: all snake dreamers are mad.

"That's enough," Pearl intervened. "You've tired her out." She ushered him to the door, then turned to her daughter. "It's time we talked," she said. "I need to know what happened. I have my story as well."

They had exchanged only a few sentences, however, when Pearl was summoned to the nursing station. Teno was on the telephone. "How is Dusa?" she asked, the doctor concerned for her patient, reasonable as always. "She has been very fortunate. The nurses tell me she is making a good recovery, but I'd like to hear from you."

Pearl felt her way. "Dusa is starting to get stronger," she said stiffly, "but I've been extremely anxious, especially since Diana Christopolis telephoned me. Teno, I've telephoned you two and three times every day for weeks now without getting through. What was my daughter doing alone in your boat in the middle of the ocean?"

"She stole our boat," said Teno, just as bluntly. "She's lucky to be alive. I'm sorry to tell you, Pearl, but Dusa has behaved in a totally irresponsible way. She broke into a locked hospital room at the clinic and moved an extremely ill patient; indeed, she disconnected the girl's intravenous drip, putting her life in danger. Not content with that, Dusa let herself be drawn into that other patient's delusional state. We warned her. We told her very clearly about the other girl's crazy beliefs. In spite of everything Yali and I have done for her, Dusa let her mind be poisoned against us."

"I know my daughter," Pearl replied stiffly. "I do not believe she is irresponsible. I have not heard her side of it, Teno, so I won't say anything more at present. You say she stole your boat. What do you intend to do about it?"

"Nothing," replied Teno, "unless you and Dusa make it necessary. I warn you, Pearl, don't let Diana talk you into anything foolish. She's a discharged employee and not to be trusted.

"Apparently the cruiser is undamaged. In other circumstances we might have asked you to compensate the men who rescued Dusa and the boat, but the girl was our responsibility, and we accept the cost. I'm sure it will come as no surprise to you that we will not have her back again.

"I have two recommendations for you, Pearl. First, encourage Dusa to talk to you, even if her words sound like the ravings of delirium. Let her tell her story. I must warn you, you will be shocked. There will be much that you cannot possibly believe. And you should not believe it, Pearl, hold fast to that! However, I feel that Dusa's long-term prognosis is excellent. The snake dreams have diminished markedly since the archaeological expedition she made with us. We've been delighted with that aspect of her progress. I venture to predict that the snakes will trouble her no longer.

"Dusa's other delusions are largely the product of another girl's unbalanced mind. Dusa will deal with them most easily with good professional help. I could recommend a psychologist or a psychiatrist in Toronto, but in light of Dusa's suspicions, that is not worth considering. Your GP will give you some names, Dr. Andrews, isn't it?" She paused.

Pearl realized she had been holding her breath, and gulped in air.

"Yali agrees with me," Teno continued, "although you are welcome to speak to her independently, now or later. Dusa has given us a great deal of anxiety. I may say, Pearl, that I have spoken to the harbor police, and I or Yali will speak to officials at the Canadian Embassy, since I understand they have been involved. We will tell them what happened, and also that we accept responsibility and that there will be no charges of any kind. As far as we are concerned, the matter is closed."

"Thank you," said Pearl faintly.

. . .

The officials shrugged and threw up their hands. Dusa felt guilty for keeping silent, but she did not even try to tell them about Lucy. What was the use? Lucy was dead.

It was easier to talk to Pearl. "This is about Gorgons," she began bravely. "Mom, to start with, you have to believe there are Gorgons." Dusa looked her question: Can you believe?

"Diana Christopolis told me that Yali and Teno were Gorgons," said Pearl quietly.

"You talked with Diana?"

"She telephoned me in Toronto. That was really why I came to Athens, though it took me a week after her call to get worked up to it."

"Did you believe Diana, about Yali and Teno?"

"Over the phone? Just like that? How could I? I don't believe people who say they've been kidnapped by aliens either!" Pearl shook her head. "But I couldn't stop thinking about it. What if she was right? Some very strange things do happen in this world. Some very strange things have happened to you. Dusa, I was afraid I'd never see you again." Pearl shuddered. They hugged each other fiercely.

The rest of the story was easier to tell. Pearl and Dusa cried together about Medusa, and about Lucy. "I know *you* believe all of this," Pearl said at last. "It did not happen to me, Dusa, but I accept it as your reality. You are not crazy. I know you are not crazy. That's as far as I can get, at least for now. Can you live with that?"

Dusa's answering smile was brilliant. Since returning to Athens, she had felt no stir from her snakes, and she had missed them. Now in her head the little snake roused contentedly, and then sank down again.

Pearl came closer to believing in Gorgons after Diana visited the hospital. "I'm sorry it took this long to meet both of you," she explained. "I'm just back from taking one of our former patients home to South Africa. Your messages were waiting. Dusa, I'm the infamous Diana. You've heard about me, I'm sure." She grinned, white teeth and a couple of gold caps gleaming in her dark face.

Dusa stared at her. "I wished you were there," she said. "I wished all of you were there." Her eyes brimmed.

Diana leaned forward. She held out her hands. Dusa took them, uncertainly at first, then with a fierce grip.

Diana's grin had vanished. "I wish I could have been there for you, Dusa," she said. "It could not happen, though, truly. I am here now. Do you want to talk about it? I want to hear anything you choose to say—your anger, fair enough—you have a right to be angry, at me, at others. Why don't you begin with that?"

Dusa did. Diana, Yali, Teno . . . Then she began to talk about Perse, and broke into violent tears. "I was mad at him too," she sobbed, "and then, and then . . . He's dead, and it's all my fault." She had tried not to think about her departure from the island or about Perse's farewell kiss. Now it came tumbling out, punctuated by bursts of tearing sobs.

Diana listened. "He's dead, and it's all your fault," she echoed.

"She's dead, she's dead." Dusa sobbed, beating her fists rhythmically against her thighs.

Diana waited. "She's dead," Diana said quietly. Her

own strong hands covered Dusa's and held them quiet. "Who is she?"

"Lucy, of course," Dusa shot back. "It's all my fault."

"That's it," said Diana, "that's what you needed to say."

Pearl shrank back in her chair. In the past few days, Dusa had often cried for her friend, but had never blamed herself. She had said a lot about Medusa, but almost nothing about Perse. Why did Dusa blame herself for Lucy's death? And for Perse's?

Dusa's sobs subsided at last.

Diana waited several minutes before she spoke. "You feel extremely guilty," she said quietly. "I understand. But, Dusa, Lucy made her choice. So did Perse."

"They died so I could get away." Dusa stared at her with tragic eyes.

"Lucy died. It's natural for you to feel guilty: you survived." She paused. "Perse risked—whatever he risked. He felt that he risked his life, I don't doubt. I give him credit for it, and so should you. For the rest, you don't know that Perse died.

"That island, Dusa, is an extremely strange place. I believe Perse was right when he told you he was bound to it, along with his father. He was sure that Medusa would try to kill him if she was revived. Was he right about that?"

"No," said Dusa, remembering. "She never wanted to kill anybody."

"Trust her, then," said Diana. "Teno and Yali would be furious, of course. Believe me, I know how furious they would be, but they wouldn't kill him either. He's too useful to them, and his father is getting old."

226

"Maybe they killed him first and thought about it afterwards." Dusa recalled those hurtling, dangerous shapes.

"No," said Diana flatly. "I know their mind games. Whatever they might try to make you think, those two never, ever lost control. You can be sure of that."

"Why didn't you take Lucy when you ran away? If you had taken Lucy, she would be alive."

"If I'd taken Lucy," said Diana, "if I'd even tried to take her, she would be dead. I got the others out of danger. Lucy was far too ill. You saw her, you must understand that. It was difficult enough to manage everything else. In seven years, that two-week trip to Toronto was the only time ever that both Dr. Gordons were away at the same time. They kept a very careful eye on me."

"They said you wanted to start your own clinic," said Dusa.

"They lied," said Diana calmly. "They are good liars. They have had a great deal of experience." She rose.

"There's a lot we haven't talked about, but that's more than plenty for now," she said. "I can't be your therapist, Dusa, much as I'd like to. I'm personally too much involved for it to work well, even if you were to stay in Greece, which you should not." She laughed, wryly. "Yali and Teno did what they promised, didn't they. The nightmares and the seizures are gone. You're cured."

Dusa nodded slowly. She did not say anything about the little snake.

The next day, Dusa left the hospital and moved into her mother's pleasant hotel room, a short block away from the sea. They opened the door to discover the navy soft-sided case and tan duffel bag that Dusa had last seen on the island!

"Who brought this luggage?" Pearl asked, but the bell captain did not recall.

He pointed to the labels: "I could see it is the right name, so I send them up." He beamed at her, obviously pleased with himself.

It was not swimming weather, but Dusa was determined to go for a walk on the beach at least once before she and Pearl flew home. First, though, she had to find out what Pearl was thinking.

Pearl knew she must be honest with her daughter. "I can't help it," she admitted. "I simply cannot believe that Medusa's head and body were buried separately for three thousand years, and then she came to life and turned poor Lucy to stone! Dusa, it's preposterous. It cannot have happened that way. They tricked you. That at least is believable, though I can't think *why*."

"Me neither," Dusa replied dryly.

"I love you, darling," said Pearl.

Dusa accepted this, but was not really satisfied. If only Pearl could see something for herself!

"What happened to the *Euryale?*" Dusa asked abruptly.

"I don't know."

"Find out, Mom, please. We need to go aboard."

"That doesn't sound like a good idea," ventured Pearl. "Why go back? Put it behind you, Dusa, isn't that best?"

"No," said Dusa. "Mom, find out, please."

The *Euryale* was at the marina, waiting for her owners. They went the following morning by taxi. It was a repeat

228

performance of that earlier trip with Yali and Teno; Dusa might have been riding in the same cab, listening to the same singer, hearing the crash of the same waves. Nothing had changed, and everything had changed. It was almost too much to bear.

In the dilapidated metal shed, the same man stood at the counter, still in his navy jacket. He remembered Dusa and gave her the key. "Same place they keep the plane," he said. "You can find?"

"Sure," said Dusa. "Thanks."

Like that earlier day, this day was sunny, though winter had set in definitely now, and the forecast threatened snow. Dusa hung tight to her mother's arm.

"I want to be sure I know what I'm doing," said Pearl. "We're looking for a piece of stone, right? A little piece of pink quartz, about as big as my finger." She looked at Dusa's white face. "Darling, you're ill! You shouldn't be here."

"I'm fine, Mom. Come and help."

On hands and knees, mother and daughter covered every inch of the main cabin. They checked the lockers. They emptied the trash. They explored the deck.

"I know it's small," said Pearl at last, "but I don't think it's here. I'm freezing. Dusa, darling, can't you tell me why this is so important to you?"

Dusa shook her head. "If we find it, I'll tell you," she said. "I suppose it could have rolled down below."

Pearl followed her down the three steps of the companionway. Again they knelt, running their hands over every inch of the floor. When they came to the vee berth, Dusa flopped dejectedly.

"Isn't that your bag?" asked Pearl, pointing at a net hammock slung along one side of the vee.

Dusa's eyes widened. Her tapes, and her little player! She had forgotten all about them. Now she emptied the bag on the bed where she had slept, and there it was: Bob Marley's *Legend*. With trembling fingers, she inserted the cassette in the player and pressed "play."

"Help me," said Lucy's voice, out of the past, "Help me if you can."

Dusa threw herself into Pearl's arms and sobbed as if she would never stop.

Later, from Toronto, Dusa tried to locate Lucy's home. Australia is a huge country, but Lucy had described a huge property, and Dusa was hungry for any information about the friend who had dared so much. Months later, the station was located, in Queensland, still in the Atherton name. Pearl helped Dusa put together a letter to the current owner, to which a reply was eventually received.

"In response to your inquiry," the owner wrote, "I regret to tell you that my brother and his wife were killed in the crash of a small plane near Athens. You ask especially about their daughter, Lucy. At the time of her parents' death, Lucy was a patient at a private clinic in Greece. She died there, not long after her parents, of heart failure. Anorexia is listed by the attending physician as a contributing cause of death.

"I'm afraid this letter must seem cold and impersonal," the writer continued. "I was out of touch with my brother and his family, and had not seen my niece for many years. Again, I'm sorry to give you such sad news."

Dusa was not in the least surprised to confirm that the attending physician had been Dr. Teno Gordon, "a very patient, reasonable physician," and that Lucy's uncle had been satisfied that his unfortunate niece had received the best of care.

Twice Dusa searched medical and psychological journals, looking for references to the Gordon sisters or new articles they had published. A cooperative reference librarian helped her to access computerized indexes. To Dusa's relief, she did not find anything. Whatever they were doing, the Gordons were no longer prominent in the treatment of adolescent sleep disorders.

Dusa and her mother still live in the little house in east end Toronto, not far from the bluffs where Dusa learned to climb. Dusa graduated with honors from high school, and will start college, on a scholarship, next year. She wants to study archaeology, and mythology, and psychology: four years isn't nearly long enough, but it will be a beginning. A continuation, rather. Dusa remembers what she has already learned. From time to time, she feels the touch of Medusa's sinewy hand. From time to time, the little snake, sapphire stripes gleaming along its black body, rouses comfortably and then settles once more in her mind.